BOUGHT

NEW YORK BROTHERHOOD

BIANCA COLE

CONTENTS

ANDREI

"*S*ir, it's time," Alexi says, sticking his head through the door into my office.

I give him a nod, and he leaves me alone. The virgin auction is tonight. As *pakhan* to the New York Brotherhood, I'm expected to attend.

I'm the youngest *pakhan* any brotherhood has ever had in North America at thirty-two years old. My lack of age and experience I compensate for with a heavy-fisted approach. The only way to retain power is to rule with an iron fist.

I was born into this life. A life I wouldn't choose for myself, but often, many aspects of life we have no control over.

This virgin auction happens every single year. I don't enjoy attending, as I always make a purchase. It helps feed the image of me as a brutal leader. I buy a virgin every year to fuck and discard. At least, that's what everyone believes.

No one is any wiser to the fact this couldn't be further from the truth. Not even Alexi, my *sovietnik*, knows the truth. If they don't want me to fuck them, I don't.

The biggest turnoff for me is a woman who doesn't want me. It makes me sick to think of the men who force themselves on these poor women. Instead, I put them to work in one of my many homes in America. Compared to the treatment they've endured over the past twelve months, life with me is a blessing.

I shut down my computer and stand from my desk chair. The full-length mirror on my office wall draws my attention. As I stare at myself, I don't recognize the man I am today.

I smooth the front of my tailored suit and adjust my tie, ensuring I look the part. A strand of my dark hair is out of place, and I slick it back. My beard could do with a trim, but I can't be assed to fuck around with it right now.

The heaviness of my position weighs on my soul, crushing what little is left. Bratva life is blood and more blood. We thrive off of hurt, pain, and deceit, which has been enough to destroy what I once was. There are remnants of who I was before, but they are in tatters, unrecognizable.

The auction happens in the city at a high-end club called Strelka—one of our clubs. We shut it down today for the auction—invitation only. Even though they belong to my brotherhood, the men who run the virgin auctions are of the lowest rank.

They love breaking young women's minds and torturing them for months. Most of the time, the women I buy can't remember who they are or the lives they led before the slavers captured them.

I walk out of my office and find Alexi waiting for me. "The car is ready for you, sir."

I give him a nod, saying nothing. He falls in step behind me, always ensuring he respects my position as the outright leader. Alexi has been a dutiful and perfect *sovietnik* to me since I became *pakhan* on my thirtieth birthday two years ago.

"Is everything in order?" I ask, not turning to look at him.

"Yes, sir. We've paid off The NYPD to ensure no disturbance this evening."

We have several contacts in the NYPD, and they're all happy to take bribes and ignore our operations. The police are as corrupt as the organized crime groups in this city — more cops than you would expect line their pockets with anything we offer them.

"Good," I say, stepping out of my Manhattan townhouse. Two of my men stand on either side of my front door and give me a nod as a show of respect.

The bustle of people walking along the sidewalk and the drone of engines flood the air. A blacked-out, armored SUV waits in my space, engine running. I open the back door and slide inside, letting my head fall against the headrest.

Alexi gets into the passenger's side. Once he's buckled in, Yakov, my driver, pulls away from the house. Strelka is a ten-minute drive, dependent on traffic, which isn't too heavy. I can't understand why I'm eager to get this over.

Public appearances aren't my favorite pastime. There's always a chance something might go wrong. This virgin auction brings *pakhans* from other North American brotherhoods of the Bratva. It's a tense, alpha-driven atmosphere. Everyone wants to be on top and prove their dominance.

There's something so debase and unrefined about the traditions of the Bratva. When my father died, I wanted to change things. However, my men advised against it.

A leader who shows mercy and disgust for our ways, the ways we've run things for years, is a leader another person can easily overthrow.

Instead, my closest brothers advised me to be brutal. Despite myself, I took the advice, knowing it was true. I'm thankful I no longer live in Russia. The last time I was there, I vowed I'd never return. It is even more reliant on the Bratva ways of life. The brutality is a step beyond what we experience here in America.

It was a blessing when the Moscow Elite drove my

father and me away from our homeland. A place I don't recognize anymore. America is my home now. I've been here since I was twenty-two years old.

We thrived here, and the current leadership of the Russian Bratva couldn't stand it. It's the reason why they assassinated my father two years ago while driving down this same street.

Bratva members from our home country had been trying to kill us ever since they drove us away. Two years ago, they succeeded.

I remember that day as if it were yesterday. The day I didn't go with him to a meeting because I was sick with a fever. A minute after he left the house, I felt the blast. Our enemies blew up his car a hundred meters down the road.

It was the worst day of my life. My father may have been the feared and powerful *pakhan* of our outfit, but he was just Dad to me. A man who had looked after me since my mother abandoned both of us early in my life.

His death only reasserted the truth he had tried to drill into me for years. An iron fist keeps control, not a soft one. His death was a defining moment for me. One that made me the man I am today. Ruthless on the outside, no matter what.

My father had a weakness, and that weakness was me. People observed how he treated me, noticing that he had a soft side. It's something I've concealed about myself, no matter the costs.

"We're here, sir," Yakov announces, pulling up in front of Strelka. I nod and get out, smoothing down my suit as I step onto the sidewalk.

Alexi is by my side in a flash, giving me an uneasy look. He's always worried about me. That's why Alexi makes the perfect *sovietnik*. I had no siblings, but he's the closest thing I have to a family.

"Let's try not to piss off any of the other *pakhans* this time," he warns.

I give him a short nod but promise nothing. The run-in at last year's virgin auction wasn't my fault. An asshole called Georgy Veselov, *pakhan* of the Miami Brotherhood, picked a fight with me.

I beat him, and that was that. He's a power-hungry idiot who thought he could beat me in a bare-knuckle fight. I've not yet met a man alive who can.

The place is heaving as I step through the doors. I despise how many people show up to spend fortunes on slavery. Most of the virgins are tourists snatched from the airport. It makes it easier for the slavers to cover their tracks. The American government can't trace foreign girls.

Rykov, the man who runs the auction, is lingering nearby. The moment he sees me, he rushes over.

I can't stand the guy, but he's part of my outfit. "Sir, I'm so glad you could make it." He bows his head.

"What are the pickings like this year?" I ask, trying to sound interested.

He smiles a vindictive smirk. "There are a couple I think you will love, including a stunning redhead." He shifts a little closer and lowers his voice. "Although she's feisty, my men haven't been able to break her, which means she may be more hassle than it's worth. I'd happily offer you a sneak preview before the auction starts." He straightens and clears his throat, noticing Luka Romanov glaring at us.

"Perfect, lead the way." I nod my head toward the stairs that lead into the basement, ignoring the Los Angeles pakhan's glares.

He scurries ahead of me into the basement.

Alexi turns to me once he's out of earshot. "Rykov is such a weasel."

"Tell me about it." I shake my head. "I've never liked him."

"See you after the preview." He claps me on the shoulder.

I descend into the dank, damp basement, which will have been home to these girls for months. Subjected to the thumping bass of the club every night for God knows how long.

It's a disgrace. These women have as many rights as us, but I know the brotherhood slavers don't distinguish. The same thing happens to men they capture. Slavery runs rife in the Bratva, and I have always longed to change that within my brotherhood.

I wait at the entrance, watching the row of fifteen women standing naked and chained together.

Rykov is speaking to the trembling, petrified woman. The flash of fiery red hair captures my attention.

A need to interrupt his pointless speech and walk toward her hits me. I want to discover more about this feisty redhead Rykov's men haven't been able to break. Instead, I grit my teeth and wait.

One girl urinates out of fear, and he flogs her. I keep my expression neutral. It grates on me to witness one of my brothers treat women this way.

This kind of brutality is lower than low. None of these women deserve this treatment, but it's the Bratva way. That's often the excuse everyone uses in these situations.

Rykov stops in front of the redhead, speaking to her, which irritates me.

"Keep your heads down. One of our most prestigious guests is here for a preview," he instructs, breaking me from my thoughts.

I walk into the room and straight for the redhead without an invitation. "Thank you, Rykov," I say.

"Sir," he replies.

I'm drawn to her like a moth to the flame. My eyes drop over her curvy, naked form. Her hourglass shape is so fucking perfect, and her breasts that I would long to suck and grope all night long.

Beautiful.

That's the only way to describe her figure. As I

stop before her, I desperately want to see her face. "Look at me," I command.

The woman shakes in front of me before lifting her chin to gaze at me. She doesn't make eye contact because it's how they've been taught. She's the most radiant woman I've ever seen. Her eyes are a bright emerald green, which complements her red hair. There's no emotion in them, though, no hatred or anger.

"I want you to look me in the eye," I command.

She hesitates for a moment before forcing her eyes to meet mine.

"*Krasivaya*," I utter.

Her eyes widen as if she understands the word, which is unusual as the virgins rarely come from Russia.

I need to remember where I am right now. I've forgotten my damn name. *Krasivaya* is the perfect word to describe her, as she is the most captivating thing I've ever seen.

The only reaction I get is the blush on her cheeks, which spread down her neck. She understands Russian.

All the blood in my body rushes south, and I lose control momentarily. Something that never happens to me.

Rykov clears his throat, breaking me from the daze I'm in.

I've been staring at her for too long, considering

I'm supposed to keep up appearances. "Return your gaze to the ground," I instruct, keeping my voice cold despite the inferno raging inside me.

She does as I say in an instance, and I walk away despite not wanting to. A wild part of me wants to claim her as mine now, offer Rykov whatever money he wants for her.

It is frowned upon for a *pakhan* to behave that way. Rykov has given me a sneak preview, which is bad enough. There's never *any* buying allowed before the auction. All *pakhans* get a fair chance at any of the virgins on offer tonight.

I regard the other women with mild interest despite being unable to get my mind off the redhead. None of them stir my interest as she does. Once finished, I walk toward the stairs to ascend back to the main room.

"I'll see you out there, sir?" Rykov asks, walking after me.

I turn and narrow my eyes at him. "Yes."

I can feel him watch after me as I walk up the stairs and into the viewing area.

There's no doubt I'm leaving with a virgin tonight, and it will be the redhead beauty. I don't care what the price is. I have to have her.

2

VERA

*T*here is a glimmer of radiant sunshine piercing through the ominous, torturous tunnel in which I find myself trapped. It has been three long years since I departed from Saint Petersburg and embarked on this journey to America, with the sole intent of being ensnared and auctioned off like a commodity. It feels like a lifetime ago, a distant memory shrouded in the depths of time.

Tonight is the night. Two years of rigorous training and one year of enslavement have led me to this esteemed event - the illustrious New York virgin auction. Only the elite members of the esteemed brotherhood from across the nation are granted the privilege to participate in this affair.

A nearby guard clears his throat, but I dare not raise my gaze. We have been taught to keep our eyes downcast, unless directly addressed.

"Look at me, suka," he spits, insulting me in Russian.

Reluctantly, I lift my gaze to meet his face, but I avoid making direct eye contact. Any form of eye contact would invite punishment. When I first arrived at the virgin camp, it took countless lashings to instill this unwavering discipline in me.

"Are you prepared to be sold tonight?" He sneers, leering over me.

"Yes, sir," I reply, my voice barely above a whisper, keeping my head bowed in submission.

He does not comprehend the depth of my readiness for this night. Revenge is tantalizingly within my grasp, and if my uncle's suspicions hold true, he will be the one to purchase me.

The man I need to buy me has an insatiable weakness for redheads, and by my uncle's machinations, I stand as the sole red-haired offering in this auction. It grants me an advantageous position, an upper hand. If he fails to bid on me, all my arduous efforts will be in vain, and I will be forced to devise an alternative plan.

"I'm sure you are, you slut. You are probably gagging for a master to take your virginity."

I ignore his words as that is all they are—empty, pointless words. All the guards take joy in degrading us with insults or pain. I learned to delight in it. As part of my training, before I arrived here, Uncle Igor taught me to endure unbelievable amounts of pain.

He chuckles and then grabs hold of my throat. "I'd love to fuck you," he says, blowing his stinking breath in my face. The lingering scent of stale cigarette smoke and alcohol turns my stomach, provoking a sickening sensation within me.

This guard absolutely despises the fact that I never show a hint of fear, no matter what he throws at me. He tightens his grip around my throat, making it hard to breathe. I stay calm. Maybe it's because I don't fear death at all.

He won't dare to kill me. It gets under the skin of every single guard in this place that I never break down, no matter how hard they try. I don't shed a tear or scream for them to stop.

I clench my teeth together as he lands a punch right in my gut. It hurts like hell, but I don't show any pain. They won't break me. The end is near.

"Time to get 'em ready!" shouts another guard.

He grabs my wrist and forces me to stand up. He unclips the chains that were holding me to the wall, and now I'm attached to one of the other virgins nearby. The men here work to line us up.

The chains rattle as they march us like cattle to the slaughter. Every night, I've dreamed of this moment, whereas the other women have been dreading it.

The girl behind me is breathing so hard, I'm worried she might pass out, and the girl in front of me is trembling with fear. I've never been more chill in the past three years.

We've been stuck together in this shithole for a whole year, and yet I don't even know their names. I recognize their faces, but we're not allowed to talk to each other.

I'm sure most of them no longer remember their names. The brutal treatment we've been through breaks us mentally and physically. It turns most into the perfect little pet for our future owners.

They think I'm ready to be sold, but they have not broken me. I believe these men have got fed up with trying. It would take much more to break my mind. The images of my family slaughtered are all I've held onto for three years. And the name of one man.

Andrei Petrov.

"Stop and turn to the side," the guard barks.

He will be here. It's a guarantee since he owns this club. The only thing out of my control is whether he will purchase me.

The slave master steps into the room, clearing his throat. I know it's him before he has spoken because of his strong tobacco scent.

"The time has come." He claps his hands together. "All of you will be auctioned off to the highest bidder. Remember your training, and don't break the rules while up on stage." There's a crack of a whip, and everyone tenses. "You don't want me to remind you what happens when you don't obey."

One girl sobs, and I hear a trickle of water. "What the fuck is wrong with you?" he growls, stampeding toward her. "What *pakhan* wants a woman who pisses herself?"

The whip cracks, and she screams as it connects with her bare flesh. We're all naked, other than a skimpy lace thong covering our innocence. "Take this one back and give her a beating. She's not ready."

I swallow hard, trying not to let their treatment of her affect me. I'm here for me and no one else. This is the Bratva way of life.

"Now, I expect the rest of you to remember your training and impress the men wanting to buy you." His footsteps come closer, and he stops in front of me. "Do you understand?"

"Yes, sir," everyone mutters.

He grips my chin between his finger and thumb hard, forcing me to look up at him. "Still not scared of me?" he asks.

I don't reply, keeping my jaw clenched tight.

He shakes his head. "Keep your heads down, as one of our most prestigious guests is here for a preview."

We all fall into submission, keeping our eyes on the ground.

"Thank you, Rykov," a deep baritone voice cuts through the room.

"Sir," the slave trader replies.

The temptation to glance at the newcomer is

great, but I keep my head bowed. His heavy footsteps echo closer and closer as I keep my eyes fixed on the ground. Another pair of shoes appear before me— expensive, polished black brogues.

A shiver runs down my spine as the man speaks, "Look at me," he commands.

I gaze at his face, keeping my attention on his face but not his eyes. A cold dread slices through me as I recognize him. The man I'm here to kill.

I school my features as my uncle has taught me to do, not allowing an ounce of emotion through the barrier. Inside, hot rage is bubbling like lava beneath the earth's rocky surface.

"Look me in the eye," he commands.

A flood of panic fills me, as it's not a usual request. Eyes are the gateway to your soul, and I can't afford him learning the truth in mine.

They are the hardest part of your body to mask, but I do as he says, keeping my glare cold even if there's a burning inferno of pure hate and rage bubbling within me.

His dark eyes are almost kind as he stares into mine. I expected ice, but they're warm. I'd seen his photos from three years ago, but he is more handsome than in those.

His hair is styled longer on the top and shorter on the sides. The only difference is that he has a neat beard that he didn't have in the photos.

However, in those photos, he was leering over my

dead family. As he keeps my gaze, I detect the passion and desire in his eyes. It's enough to make me sick to the stomach.

This man murdered my entire family in cold blood. He's the reason I've endured all this pain. The reason I'm here is to end him once and for all.

"*Krasivaya*," he utters.

My eyes widen for half a second. The shock of hearing Andrei utter that word about me. There's a pulse of something between us as we stare at each other, silence falling for longer than it should.

Rykov clears his throat.

It seems to break Andrei's attention. "Return your gaze to the ground," he orders the cold and commanding tone back in place.

I do as he says. I'm itching to wrap my fingers around his throat and choke the life out of him. It figures they would give him an early viewing of the offerings. The man has never been to this auction and has not bought a virgin. The first year, he purchased one under his father's instruction but has upheld it since his death two years ago. He no doubt fucks them and discards them once he's taken their virginity.

He doesn't ask other girls to look at him, making me sure he will pick me. The plan is going as I'd expected up to now. It is minutes until we will be paraded onto the stage and sold.

"I'll see you out there, sir?" Rykov asks. For the

first time, I've learned the name of the man who has beaten us into submission.

"Yes," he says before leaving the room.

My breathing has sped up, and so has the usually steady beat of my heart. The encounter with Andrei before the auction is something I didn't foresee. I was ready to walk onto that stage and for him to buy me. I was not expecting such a close encounter with him before it.

For the first time since they took me into the virgin camps, he has rattled me. It feels like that one encounter has sent me spinning off course, and I'm not as grounded as I was minutes earlier.

I shut my eyes and try to control myself, remembering my training. My uncle's voice sounds in my head on repeat.

*Breathe and picture your goal in your min*d.

I do that, forcing myself to bring my emotions under control. Up to now, my training has all been theoretical.

I've never been confronted with the emotions that flooded me when I looked into his eyes—a monster's eyes. But it will take much more than an unexpected visit from Andrei Petrov to derail me.

So much more…

3

ANDREI

I can't keep my attention off the gorgeous redhead bound in metal on the stage—the eighth year I've been to this auction, but the second without my father.

He insisted that we purchase a virgin each year but that we present them with a choice. They would be allowed to stay at our New York residence and sleep with me or be put to work in one of our other homes in North America as a cleaner or cook, depending on the woman's skill sets.

He would even afford them a wage and allow them to reside in the servants' quarters. It never concerned me one way or the other if they wished to sleep with me or not. I've never been hard up in that department. Even so, since my father's death two years ago, I've upheld the tradition.

My father was a good man, perhaps too good. He

never wanted the virgins. After my mother left him, he had little interest in any romantic or sexual relationship.

This virgin is the first and only woman who has captured my attention at one of these auctions in eight years. I turned to steel in my boxer briefs when her striking green eyes found mine in the holding room.

There's a power in her I've never seen before in previous offerings at these auctions. Her eyes held a steely fire, barely discernible beneath the mask she sought to hide behind.

It's a sexy quality that makes me hope she desires to be mine once I buy her. There's no doubt in my mind she is the *one* this year.

Her red hair is as hot as the fires burning in hell, and her eyes are as beautiful as polished emerald gems. The notion of dominating her body makes me wild with need. I long to see her tied down to my spanking bench in my pleasure room at home.

I'd turn her white skin a perfect red, alternating between spanking her and pleasuring her until she couldn't take it anymore.

Fuck.

My cock throbs and my balls tingle as I keep my eyes on her. It pisses me off that they control the women, forcing them to keep their heads bowed. I want to gaze into her eyes again — those beautiful, bright green eyes.

Will she even remember her name?

The expression in her eyes that the girl tried so hard to mask suggests she hasn't been broken mentally by the torture. It means Rykov was telling the truth when he admitted they hadn't been able to break her, as he knows I lean toward feisty women.

Perhaps she has managed to hold onto her memories, unlike the previous woman I've purchased. I wanted to hear her voice, but it's something I couldn't ask for—not in front of the *shestyorka*.

They may be the lowest rank in our brotherhood, but they're not stupid. A show of weakness is too much of a risk. I can't break the rules in front of them.

They are parading around a dark-haired Asian girl at the moment. I wince at the sight of bruises on the back of her legs as she turns. I find my eyes flicking to the beauty I'm so taken with.

A brief scan of her body reveals the extent of the damage. I hadn't noticed the wounds in the dark holding room. Her flawless skin is marred with minor, superficial bruises. They never break the skin, careful to make sure the virgins aren't permanently scarred.

I can't figure out why her injuries bother me so much. The tension in my jaw makes it ache as I force myself to look anywhere but at her. No one would ever hurt her in my house.

My attention returns to the girl on the stage, commanding a bidding war. Two Brotherhood men are going head to head for the woman they want. The auction has struck five million dollars, and it is still rising.

It's no use trying to keep my eyes off the woman I crave, so I return all my attention to *my* redhead, wondering what she will cost.

She's by far the most beautiful woman on that stage. A possessiveness claws at me as I keep my attention fixed on her. I hate that the other men in the room can see her naked. She's a virgin that I wouldn't mind deflowering and making mine.

Something tells me if I bedded her, I wouldn't be able to let her go. My days of virgin purchasing would be *over,* even though I never purchased them to deflower, anyway. It's all a show my father believed essential to uphold as *pakhan.*

Rykov steps forward, signaling for everybody to be silent. "Last lot is number fifteen."

My heart gallops as the redhead steps forward. I straighten, observing her. Although I keep my outward appearance unaffected, I'm a mess inside.

There are murmurs of appreciation as a handful of men reach for their paddles — hot possessiveness coils through my gut.

None of them can outbid me. It's not possible. The New York Brotherhood is the largest and richest, which means I have more money than any of them. I'd pay any price for her.

Not only because it asserts my dominance as the

New York brotherhood *pakhan* but because I want her. For some inexplicable reason, I want her badly.

My paddle is in my hand the moment the bidding starts. I keep it down, waiting while the bidding increases. There's no use getting an arm ache when I expect this to go into the multi-millions.

The lower-ranking bidders drop out as the bid reaches seven million dollars. The sum is too much now for anyone but a *pakhan*.

Once there are only two left, I lift my paddle. One guy drops out, bowing his head in defeat. I meet the gaze of the other guy, Luka Romanov, and he glares at me. He's the *pakhan* of another brotherhood running out of Los Angeles. This will be a hard fight, but I'm confident I'll win.

He keeps going, driving the auction up to eleven million dollars. I gaze back at the redhead, who is unmoving and appears unaffected by the fact she's being sold for an obscene sum of money. I haven't splashed out too much on my virgins in previous years, but this time, I must.

Luka is turning a deeper red by the second. I just bid fourteen million dollars without even batting an eyelid. I've got too much money to know what to do with it, anyway. What's a few million more?

He bids another two hundred thousand.

"Fifteen million dollars," I say, not wishing to go up in such insignificant sums of money anymore. I will win. I always do.

No matter what, I will leave with this woman. If she goes for one hundred million dollars, I will pay for it. I'm not sure why. Perhaps it's because she reminds me of myself—broken but strong despite everything.

Luca sets down his paddle, glowering at me with a fiery hatred. He doesn't concern me. The brotherhood in Los Angeles is nothing compared to my outfit.

"Lot fifteen goes to Andrei Petrov."

I return my gaze to my prize, noticing the tension in her shoulders ease. It makes little sense, considering she doesn't know who I am or who has bought her.

Maybe she's glad it is over. She can't understand how lucky she is that I've purchased her instead of Luka. Luka is one of the worst kinds of *pakhan*. He's renowned for enjoying torturing, and it's believed he murdered his late wife a few years back.

A young woman is sitting by his side, keeping her gaze down. She is his daughter, as far as I'm aware. It shows what kind of man he is, bringing his daughter to an event like this. It is sick.

The redhead is the last lot of the evening, and people stand from their seats to leave. A tension coils through my muscles as Luka and his *sovietnik*, Miron, walk toward me. "Andrei, a good fight for the redhead."

I nod my head. "No hard feelings, I hope? I hadn't snapped one up yet, and I always get a virgin at this auction."

He pats me on the back. "Of course not. All is a fair fight, and I backed out when you got too rich for my blood." His eyes narrow. "If you'd excuse me." I watch as Luka walks away to join his daughter—she can't be much older than eighteen.

Miron lingers behind. "How have you been, Andrei?"

I give the man a respectful nod, remembering our time working together in Russia in my late teens. He's one of the more honorable guys of the other brother-hoods. "I'm well, thank you. How are you?"

He shrugs. "I'm as well as can be expected while attending this disgusting event," he says, keeping his voice quiet. "I'm sure you agree with my opinions, even if you wouldn't like to admit it."

I eye the man, keeping quiet. I could not have said it better myself, but I can't voice my opinion—not here. It doesn't matter who is asking me. "It was good seeing you, Miron. Take care." I turn away and walk toward the stage. My prize is waiting for me to collect her.

The most beautiful virgin I've ever acquired. I can't deny that as I walk to claim her, I'm hoping she is the second one to opt for me to take her virginity. However, it's unlikely. Six out of the seven I've purchased thus far opted to work in one of my house-holds. If statistics are anything to go by, it's unlikely she will want to be with me.

"Andrei, are you ready to complete your transaction?" Rykov asks, popping up from nowhere.

The man is a snake. He may be part of my brotherhood, but he is one of the lowest of the low in our brigades. The day of the auction is the only time I interact with him.

"I'm ready," I say, walking toward the stairs to the dungeon he'd led me into earlier.

He doesn't utter another word as he walks behind me, taking his rightful place. Even though he's a cocky son of a bitch, he's got the good sense to keep quiet around me. I'm sure he knows how much I dislike him.

The fast patter of my heart thuds in beat with my footsteps as I make my way to my virgin. I can't understand why she has affected me so much.

"You've picked a tough one, sir. None of my men have been able to break her. It's a first," Rykov says, speaking from behind.

I glance back at him. "I'm sure I'll be able to change that," I say, clenching my jaw.

He smirks at me, eyes lighting with a sick joy that makes my stomach churn.

It feels wrong to utter those words about her, but it's what I'm expected to say. I won't break her, but I damn well hope she wants me in the same way that I want her. I'm worried that if she doesn't, I may not be able to let her go. Only time will tell.

THE BEAUTY I've purchased sits unmoving by my side in the car. She has yet to glance up from her lap, staring at her hands clasped together. It's how she has been taught by the men who groomed her for the auction.

I have every intention of breaking her out of these ridiculous habits. I grab her hand and squeeze, making her tense. "You need not be afraid of me."

She tries to pull her hand away, stunning me. These virgins are typically calmer. There's something about this fiery redhead that I can't put my finger on. She's different—special.

Rykov already made it clear his men hadn't broken her. It makes me long for her more. A woman so strong and so beautiful, who deserves to be treated well—like a princess.

"I won't treat you the way those men treated you." I let my finger trace her cheek gently, pushing a stray hair away from her eyes and tucking it behind her ear.

"Why not?" she asks.

My eyes widen at the question. It's bold, considering the girl is at the mercy of a man who purchased her. "I'm not the monster people believe me to be," I say, searching her bright green eyes.

She doesn't appear too convinced by my statement. Her eyes are as hard as emerald jewels. There's no emotion in them, not even a whisper of fear. She is a mystery to me — an enigma wrapped in the most tempting package. Something so unusual about her, and I want to dig my way under the surface and find out what it is. What makes this woman tick?

"You will soon learn what kind of man I am."

Her eyes flash with something so quickly that I can barely register it.

Yakov comes to a stop outside of my house and slides down the privacy screen. "We're here, sir."

I clear my throat and steal a glance at my town-house. "Thank you, Yakov." I get out of my side of the car and walk around to her side. She stares at me blankly as I open the door for her. "Out."

She jumps out of the car onto the pavement, and I grab her hand as a precaution. The last thing I need is an escaped virgin. She tenses the moment I touch her as if I've electrocuted her with my skin. This woman is impossible to read. She doesn't show any fear but flinches when I touch her.

I lead her into the house, shutting the front door behind us. Once inside, she pulls her hand away and hugs her arms around herself. A defensive move, which is no doubt a result of the shit those assholes put her through in that rotten club.

I hate to think of her in that basement for however many months with them. It makes me feel sick. "I'll show you to your room," I say, nodding toward the staircase.

She follows me cautiously as I walk up the stairs and turn left to her room, adjoining mine. However, I won't tell her that yet. First, I need to find out if she is interested in staying. I stop outside the room and glance back at her. "This will be your room." I open the door to the lavish, large room with a feminine touch since my housekeeper, Olga, decorated it. It's a little smaller than mine, but not by much.

She doesn't react as she glances around the room. I can't tell whether she likes it or dislikes it. A wall of ice is erected around her, making her more of a mystery to me by the second.

"Is this suitable?" I ask, wanting some response from her.

She nods her head, meandering around the edge of the room. I watch her as she lets her finger run through the silk bedding on the four-poster bed.

The dominant side of me wants to throw her onto it and take her without her permission. A sick and twisted part of me that lives deep within, rearing its ugly head the moment I set eyes on her. She makes me crazy.

"I'll leave you to rest for a while." She keeps her back to me while I talk. "I'll be back to fetch you for a late dinner."

She doesn't turn around, and I don't demand that she does. Instead, I force myself to walk out of that room before I do something I regret.

I've never had trouble keeping myself in control

around the virgins purchased before. Six of them never even slept with me, but the thought of never being inside the red-haired beauty on the other side of the door makes me hot with rage and possession.

She will be my greatest challenge yet for more than one reason.

4

VERA

y finger teases along the sharp edge of the straight-edge razor I found in the bathroom cabinet. The blade is for cutting a beard but would cut a man's throat easily. It's so sharp. The thought of cutting Andrei's throat with this razor makes my heart dance with excitement.

However, on the precipice of revenge, a quick and easy death seems too anti-climactic. Three years I've spent training and getting ready for this moment. There is not enough justice in this being over within a day of my arrival.

I know the brotherhood will kill me the moment I carry out my task. It will be worth giving my life for, though. My life is nothing anymore. The moment that man murdered my family was the moment I stopped living.

Andrei left me alone in this bedroom, giving me

the chance to find the razor. He has yet to learn who I am and what I intend to do. The sound of footsteps approaching the room has me flinging the knife under the pillow on the bed.

I kneel, staring at the floor—the position expected of slaves when anyone enters the room.

The door swings open, and the man I loathe steps inside. "I wanted to come and check on you." I can see his shoes in front of me. "Please don't act this way around me," he says when the door shuts behind him.

My brow furrows, and I keep my eyes on the floor. "How do you wish me to act, sir?"

He clears his throat. "I want you to stand in my presence as an equal. I want you to look me in the eye and speak to me as if I'm a normal person." He steps closer and lowers his voice. "As if you weren't a slave."

A request I will find challenging. The detachment and coldness of interactions between slave and master would make this easier for me. If he expects me to act civil around him, it will be more of a struggle to mask my disdain for him.

"Look at me," he commands.

I force my chin up and meet his dark, hot gaze. The desire burning in his eyes makes my stomach churn. All the things I've sacrificed to this point, I've managed to hold onto my virginity. The thought of handing my innocence over to a man I loathe makes me sick, particularly a man who has taken everything from me this far.

"Are you comfortable?" he asks.

I will be once you're dead.

I nod my head, unable to speak.

He reaches out to touch me, tracing a line across my cheek with such tenderness it makes me shudder.

"I wish to offer you a choice, but we will discuss the matter over dinner." He nods his head toward a door in the wall. "You have clothes in there." His eyes return to mine, and he holds my gaze. "Dress and meet me at the bottom of the stairs." He doesn't wait for an answer, turning and leaving me staring after him.

Everything had been going as I expected until this moment. Andrei Petrov isn't beating me or acting brutally toward me. His actions are unsettling. As fucked up as that is, I want him to beat me and act the way I expected. I want him to act the way I planned. For the first time since I found my family dead, I'm unsettled. He hasn't even got any guards watching over me.

Why would he have dinner with a sex slave he spent millions of dollars on? Perhaps he is trying to put me at ease before savagely taking my virginity like the monster he is.

I try to push the anxiety from my mind, focusing on my goal. There's no rush. I'm here with him now, and three years leading to this can allow a few days to decide how I want to exact my revenge. It has to be something fitting — the need to make him hurt as much as I did clawing at me.

I step toward the closet and open the door. It's a walk-in wardrobe filled with expensive, designer women's clothes. The clothes and shoes would excite most women, but they don't interest me. He probably keeps these clothes here for every virgin he buys. My fingers tease at the expensive silk fabric of a black maxi dress that catches my eye. I pull it from the hanger and slip it on, finding it fits me.

There is a floor-to-ceiling mirror, and I gaze at my reflection. I don't recognize myself at all. My face is paler than when I last looked in a mirror. I'm thinner than before the New York Brotherhood captured me. As I look into my eyes, I can still see myself. My resolve and passion are driving me forward. Revenge is all I want, the only thing I have craved since that day.

I step out of the closet, shutting the door behind me. The razor remains under my pillow, and I grab the hilt, folding the blade and tucking it into my bra cup. The thought of being unarmed around is too dangerous. After one last glance in the mirror, I leave the room and approach the grand, sweeping staircase.

In another world, I would be a princess entering the large, exquisite hallway, which could be a ballroom. Andrei is waiting like my Prince Charming in a tailored suit.

In reality, life is anything but a fairytale, and those comparisons couldn't be further from the truth. Andrei stands with his back to me, but when he hears the clink of my heels on the travertine floor, he turns to face me.

He has a whiskey glass in his hand, and his eyes widen as he takes in my appearance. I watch as he sets the glass on a side table, slipping his hands into his pants pockets. His movement draws my attention to the bulge at his crotch, making me sick.

The fact he desires me in that way makes my stomach churn. The thought of having this man inside of me is wrong on so many levels.

"*Krasivaya*," he says once I'm close to him, surprising me with the word again.

A complimentary word that no brother should ever use for someone like me. It means beautiful, and it's a word with respectful connotations, which makes little sense coming from him. He grabs my hand and kisses the back of it, keeping eye contact.

Despite my repulsion, I keep my facial expression neutral.

"Follow me," he says, letting go of my hand.

He leads me down a lavish corridor lined with expensive paintings. The place is magnificently decorated, but I can't admire them. The nerves twisting my gut make it impossible to focus on anything other than the cold metal against my breast. Images of driving it deep into his skull or slicing it through his throat flash through my mind.

He stops in front of a door and opens it. "After you," he says.

I swallow hard, doing as he says and stepping into the room. The room is small and intimate—not what I had expected from a man like him. A round dining table takes center in the room, dressed in a red table-cloth. The room is bathed in romantic candlelight, which doesn't fit this situation.

It is a dinner set for a romantic couple. It makes the whole situation even more sickening, considering the real setup between us. He has purchased me as a virgin to fuck. There's nothing romantic about it. I wait for his command, standing by the door with my hands behind my back. The cold of the metal razor in my bra cup reminds me I could always pull it on him.

"Take a seat." Andrei gestures toward the seat closest to the door.

At least it will offer me an escape route. I sit and fold my hands in my lap, keeping my gaze down.

He sits opposite me. "Do you have a name?" he asks.

Ice-cold dread freezes the blood flowing through my veins. The virgins are supposed to have forgotten their names, and admitting I haven't may be dangerous.

"I know you're supposed to forget, but I get a feeling you're stronger than most," he says.

I nod my head.

"What is your name?"

"Vera," I say, so quiet I'm not sure he will hear.

He smiles, and it reaches his eyes. "Vera, so they didn't break you."

It's more of a statement, but I shake my head. I glance down at the plate before me, my stomach rumbling. It has a metal cover over it.

"I want to cut to the chase, Vera," he says, placing his palms against the table. "I bought you at the virgin auction, but I don't desire fucking a woman who doesn't want me." His eyes narrow, and he stares at me for a few beats. "If you don't wish to explore being my submissive, I will offer you employment at one of my other residences."

Shit.

This is not going to plan at all. Andrei is supposed to treat me like shit like everyone else has to this point. If I don't agree to be his submissive and give him my virginity, he will ship me off somewhere else. I need to be close to him to carry out my revenge.

The cold of the knife against my breast is calling to me. Perhaps I will have to attempt this sooner than I thought. Igor's words still resonate in my mind.

He's a monster. A beast who can't be tamed. The man who killed your family.

As I sit opposite him, I'm struggling to put the two

together. He seems too refined for cold-blooded murder. Yet, I have seen the images. The pictures of him standing over my parents' and siblings' bodies, knife in hand.

As I don't say a word, he runs a hand through his hair. "I know you've been through a lot, Vera." He shakes his head. "You need not decide right away. I want to clarify that I desire you far more than any woman I've bought." He sighs. "You're the eighth and six women who came before you opted for employment at one of my residences." He lifts the lid off his plate, revealing a steak beneath it. "Eat," he commands.

I'm speechless, wondering why he would tell me this. The man is *pakhan* to the New York Brotherhood. He can't show mercy, not to a virgin he purchased for a hideous sum of money. It makes no sense.

"Don't be shy. Eat, Printsessa." *Princess* in Russian. I wonder why he would call me that. I'm a slave, for God's sake. I couldn't be further from a princess, as he turned me into his possession the moment he bought me.

I reach for the handle and pull it off, glancing down at the thick steak and a side of mashed potatoes. My stomach growls at the sight. All we've eaten is salad and bread for twelve months.

My mouth salivates as the scent wafts around me, and the sight makes me dizzy.

I eye the man sitting opposite me before lifting my

knife and fork. The need to control the situation is making me uneasy. It's the first time I don't know what will happen next. I predict everything with precision in other cases.

The plan is veering off course because the man they have sent me to kill isn't acting the way they informed me he would.

Andrei Petrov is proving unpredictable, and I don't do unpredictable.

5

ANDREI

I watch her intently as she eats, meticulously cutting the steak into tiny, bite-sized pieces and savoring each morsel. It amazes me how she takes her time, chewing slowly and thoughtfully. I finished my steak what feels like ages ago, yet she's still not halfway through hers. The silence between us grows, almost suffocating.

I yearn to engage her in conversation, to express the intense desire I have to dominate her. But deep down, I know that pushing her would be unwise. With her, I find it difficult to decipher her thoughts and emotions.

In the past, the women I've been with were often grateful when I revealed my desires to them. They would become calm, relaxed, and even talkative. But she's different. Tension radiates from her, and she seems unmoved by the truth. Perhaps she believes it's some kind of trick.

I'm aware of the terrible abuse that women like her endure during their training to become ready for their masters. It's a reality that weighs heavily on me, knowing the pain and suffering they have endured. As I observe her picking at another minuscule bite of steak, I decide to break the silence.

"How is your steak?" I inquire, my gaze fixed on her.

She barely glances at me. "Good, thanks."

I want to hear her speak more, but she's not talk-ative. Her voice is heavenly. There's a part of me that wants to assert my dominance and insist she lay with me—I own her. It's just not my way, and I will not change that because of some weird primal need for her.

"Do you have any idea what option you might choose?" I ask.

Inside, I'm panicking about her answer. If she tells me she wants to work elsewhere, it will make me crazy. Putting her to work here would be far more tempting and seducing her. The thought of another man claiming her innocence makes me sick.

She blinks at me twice, seemingly contemplating my question, before shrugging her shoulders. "I don't understand why I have a choice," she confesses, her gaze fixed on the steak on her plate.

I can't help but smile at that. "Because I don't like

to fuck women who don't want it." I shrug. "That, and I stand firmly against the concept of slavery."

"That seems peculiar," she remarks, absentmindedly picking at her steak.

It wasn't large, but she won't be able to eat it all at this rate. It will take forever. It's often the same with the girls I get from the auction. They've consumed tiny amounts of food during their capture.

"In what way?" I ask, tilting my head to the side.

"You've just purchased a slave and funded the entire trade."

I smile at her observation but leave it hanging between us. She need not learn that my attendance and purchase is a way of maintaining my public image as the brutal pakhan I'm thought to be.

"Where are you from?" I ask, changing the subject.

"I don't know." She keeps her gaze averted, and I know she's lying.

Why would she lie to me?

She told me her name, which she could remember. There's an ever-so-slight twinge of a Russian accent to her voice, but she's trying to mask it. Her American accent is practiced and almost credible.

She knows where she is from but doesn't want to tell me.

I laugh. "Fine, keep your secrets."

She tenses, turning to ice in her chair.

What is with this woman?

There's something unusual and intriguing about her, something I can't quite put my finger on. I shift in my seat under her watchful, intense gaze. It's a little baffling, considering the men who trained her not to make eye contact.

"How old are you?" I ask.

She straightens before answering, "I'm twenty-four."

I don't let her see the surprise at learning her age. She seems older, somehow. Not because she looks old, but there's a strength in her I'd never expect from a girl of her age.

What has she been through to make her so hardened?

"Come here," I command, holding a hand out.

She swallows before standing and walking toward me.

"Take my hand."

She gives me a hesitant look before entwining her fingers with mine. A hot desire spreads through me as we touch, setting my skin on fire. I know she senses it, too, as her eyes widen. I pull her onto my lap, forcing her to sit on my knee.

She gasps, glancing at me with her hands folded in her lap.

I run my hand through her red hair and gaze into her eyes. "How did a girl as beautiful as you stay a virgin for so long?"

Tension ripples through her, and she sinks her teeth into her bottom lip. "I don't know, sir."

I shake my head. "Call me Andrei for the moment."

Her sparkling green eyes flood with confusion, and she doesn't respond. My eyes fall to her full, luscious lips, and my cock throbs in my pants. Ever since she sat down to dinner, I've been harder than stone.

The dress she picked is more than a little revealing, allowing me a perfect view of her full cleavage. I pull her close to me, lacing my fingers behind her head.

Her eyes remain blank and unfeeling. There's something this girl is hiding, as I can feel it in my bones. She's been through a lot and learned how to mask her emotions.

With one tug, her lips are on mine. I kiss her gently, but she tenses in my arm, resisting at first. After a few moments of persistence, she gives in and allows me to kiss her. My tongue delves into her mouth, searching it with a wild passion.

I'm unsure if she is giving in because she enjoys it or sticking to her training. Either way, I relish the taste of her. I can read most people like a book, but she's impossible to figure out. I bet she gave the *shestyorka* a hard time. It makes me even more excited to claim her in every way if she agrees.

I let go of the back of her neck, freeing her.

She leans away from me, eyes wide. The pretty pink staining her cheeks is cock stirring, and her irises dilate with desire. I hold her, sensing she wants to get off my lap. Even if she doesn't want to reveal that I turn her on, I do.

"I would like an answer by tomorrow, Vera."

She gazes down at her hands, chest heaving. "Either I stay here with you as your sex slave, or I live elsewhere and do housework at one of your other homes. Is that correct?" she asks, clarifying her options.

"You wouldn't be my sex slave. I would treat you with respect and allow you freedom, but you would need to allow me to dominate you in bed." I narrow my eyes at her. "I know you won't be familiar with bondage, being a virgin." I let my hands slip to her hips and dig my fingertips in. "I'd be sure to ease you into it."

She shifts in my lap, making me even harder.

"But, it is something I crave with any sexual partner," I add.

She tenses. "Sexual partner?"

I chuckle. "I like to think you would be my sexual partner, yes." I stand with her and lift her.

Her knees shake as I return her to the ground.

"Sleep on it and give me an answer in the morning," I say, setting my hand on the small of her back and guiding her out of the room. "I'm sure you are exhausted."

She says nothing, letting me escort her out of the dining room and toward the stairs. We walk together in silence across the vast entrance hall. I let her walk first up the stairs, following her. It's impossible not to admire her from behind in her tight, form-hugging dress.

Once we reach the top of the stairs, she turns toward me, lacing her fingers together.

I step close to her. "Goodnight, Vera." I kiss her cheek. "Please retire to your room," I say, nodding toward the doorway.

Her eyes widen, and she searches for something. It takes me a moment to realize she's expecting an armed escort. "No guards here. You are free to roam the house, but you won't be able to leave."

She stares at me for a long moment, judging my seriousness. After a long moment of silence, she speaks, "Good night, sir."

I grab her hand, forcing her close. "I told you to call me Andrei," I say, letting my breath tease over her lips. She is so close I could taste her again, but I don't want to push. She still has to make her choice, and pushing might make her choose to leave.

My fingers are itching to wrap around her soft, long neck. I give in to the temptation, letting my fingers tease over her skin at her throat. "Do you understand?"

She nods her head, eyes wide. Still, there's no fear in them. Everyone fears me, and I'm not used to this reaction. I close my fingers around her throat, and she doesn't bat an eyelid. "Let me hear you say it."

"I understand, si—Andrei."

I smile and give her an appreciative nod. "Good girl, now get some rest."

She gives me an odd bow before turning to leave. It's impossible not to watch how her hips sway as she walks in that tight dress. My heart pounds faster as she slips inside her room, leaving me — my cock aches in protest. The primal desire to grab her hips and force my cock inside of her tight body is so clawing it feels like I might combust.

A virgin so pure and so fucking beautiful next door to me, sleeping on the other side of a wall. I hope she agrees to be my submissive. The pleasure I'd get from her submission and forcing a reaction out of her body would be beyond satisfying.

Can I break through those walls she has erected?

The darkness she hides behind those walls will be great. I've been through terrible things, and I'm painfully aware of what it is like. I've always hated the life I was born into and that I must be the man I am today. Or, more to the point, the monster I am today.

Behind it all, there are secrets too dark to unveil. I can't understand why I'm desperate to discover what makes Vera tick. She's more intriguing to me now than when I purchased her.

She will be my most exciting conquest yet. A mystery I long to solve.

6

VERA

*T*he pain constricts around my throat as I sob into my pillow. It's almost impossible to catch my breath as the tears come so fast. For the first time in three years, my task has overwhelmed me.

The slavers beat and degraded me for months, but it was nothing compared to what I endured tonight. Sitting and eating dinner with the man who killed my family was too much. Not to mention kissing him. Andrei Petrov is the man I loathe and have to kill.

Why isn't he acting like the man I've heard so much about? Igor, my uncle, is counting on me to end his life. His words are repeating in my mind.

You are our savior, Vera. The woman who will free us from monsters like him and avenge my brother's death.

When Andrei kissed me, my body betrayed me. The shame of it crushes me. His hard muscles pressed against me, holding me, made me want to moan. I didn't, though. I kept my reactions in check, as I've been taught. When he touched me, it was like pure lightning striking me.

I hate myself for enjoying his skin on mine. I couldn't stop my reactions. He's the first man who has ever touched or kissed me before. His lips on mine were gentle but commanding. When I returned to the room, I had to dash for the bathroom and throw up that delicious steak. The emotions warring inside of me are almost impossible to get a handle on.

The soft bed does little to comfort me. I long to be back under the slaver's capture. At least I felt in control. It would always be hard, coming face to face with my family's killer. Now, he has given me an impossible choice. Throw everything I've worked for away and let him ship me off, or be his submissive. It's the only way to allow me enough time to get my revenge on him.

Uncle Igor insisted I had to kill him quickly. Hundreds of people will celebrate my sacrifice, and I'd be a hero, but I never longed for that. I want the man to suffer the way I've suffered. It means my only option is to be his submissive.

That is dangerous. The thought of allowing a man I want to kill inside of my body is a step too far. It would be worse if my body reacted the way it did to his kiss. Yet, I've got no choice. I can't let him ship me away.

There are heavy footsteps outside of my door, and I stop sobbing. The realization that I've been too loud struck me. I hold my breath, listening for movement. The sound of the doorknob turning has me reaching for the knife on the bedside table. I stow it under my pillow, ready to use it.

"Vera?" Andrei asks, his voice husky and quiet.

I remain still and unmoving, too scared to say a word.

"I heard you crying. Are you okay?" Andrei asks, stepping closer to me.

It's uncharacteristic for this man. A show of concern isn't right. His face comes into view as he steps into the moon's light, shimmering through the window. I hate that the first thought I have at the sight of his face is how handsome he is.

I can't let him see my weakness. No one sees me crying, ever. I school my features and try to make it look like I haven't cried for hours.

My mouth dries as I let my gaze drop — Andrei's wearing nothing but tight boxer briefs. The pitter-patter of my heart accelerates as he shifts into the bed by my side. Out of instinct, I shuffle away from him.

The razor is still under my pillow. I shift my eyes toward the pillow, wondering if I should make my move. Maybe Uncle Igor is right. A swift killing will ensure nothing could go wrong.

"Don't worry, I won't hurt you or try anything," he mutters. "I want to hold you."

I shiver as he wraps his muscular arms around my waist, pulling me into him. As it did before, my body reacts. I heat as his skin touches mine — a pure desire burning deep in a dark part of me. Shame is beyond what I'm feeling now. I make myself sick with the way I react. My panties are becoming damp between my thighs.

"You're safe with me," he murmurs.

I want to scream and shout. I want to slash open Andrei's throat right here and now.

Safe with a murderer. No one is safe around this man. My family is proof of that. I block out everything and go to my happy place. I draw on a childhood memory, playing in a stream with my brother and sister.

I pretend that I'm there and nothing has changed, shutting my eyes and forgetting about the man whose arms I'm in. He can't break me. No one can.

I won't let him throw me off track. I fall asleep, knowing it's my only respite from the hell I'm in.

MY EYES ARE sore and dry as I wake. I open one eye to find it's bright with sunlight in my room. The brightness burns my retinas, and I snap them shut. Then, memories of the night before flood back to me.

I sit up straight and glance toward the other side of the bed, thankful he isn't still here.

The last thing I wanted last night was for him to join me. My sobbing had kept him up, which meant his bedroom must not be far away. His irritating kindness is proving a complication I didn't foresee.

As I lay by his side last night, I could have slit his throat. My fingers tease under the pillow, searching for the razor, but it's not there. My eyes widen, and I search the room, looking for it. A chuckle from the bathroom door makes me jump. "Are you looking for this?" Andrei asks.

I glance over at him; he's holding the razor I'd been searching for in his hand, and his beard looks neater. My eyes drop, and I find he's wearing only a towel wrapped around his waist. My stomach tightens, and pussy aches at the sight of his chiseled chest with rivulets of water dripping down his skin. The way his Adonis belt carves his hips, disappearing down toward whatever he is hiding beneath that towel. I hate that I wonder what's beneath the towel.

I shake my head in response, bowing my head. He has already found the razor, and I expect punishment. I keep my eyes down as I prepare myself for the pain.

"Look at me, Vera."

I swallow hard, glancing at him.

He has placed the razor on a side table and is closer now. I watch him as he shifts to sit on the edge of the bed, still wrapped in his towel. The way his muscles flex forces me to shut my eyes, unable to keep looking at him like this. "I know you've been through awful things under the slavers, but you need not fear that treatment from me." He sets a hand on mine, making me even more confused.

I start away, pulling my hand from his.

"Vera, I hope you can learn to trust me." He sets his hand on his lap. "If not, you can go to one of my other homes. There is an opening at my house in Miami."

Miami sounds like heaven, but I can't abandon my plan. I will have to play along with being his submissive. I know that means I might have to give my virginity to him.

Again, his actions don't ring true to my expectations. He exacts no punishment for taking the razor and keeping it under my pillow. He stands from the side of the bed, turning around and unwrapping the towel, making me heat with need.

He pulls on a pair of clean boxers and then returns to the cabinet, grabbing the razor off it. I focus my attention on him as he walks toward me. "Keep the razor if it makes you feel safer." He hands me the razor.

I stare at him in disbelief, wondering why he would give me the knife. He's so confident that I wouldn't try to hurt him. Perhaps I've underestimated how easy it would be to kill him. He is a power-ful *pakhan*.

"I don't wish to push, but I wondered what your thoughts are on my offer?" He turns to face me, dark eyes burning with desire.

A shudder runs from my head to my toes, indeci-sion plaguing me. Am I capable of taking another life? I nod my head, knowing I can't fail my uncle. He's counting on me, and he told me the conse-quences of failure—It's not an option.

"Yes, I wish to remain here as your submissive," I say, keeping my gaze on the floor.

There's real joy sparkling in his eyes as he walks toward me, smiling. "That's great," he says, cupping my chin and forcing me to look at him. "I will treat you well, Vera. You've got nothing to fear."

My stomach churns as his lips near mine. My task would be far easier if he were unattractive and old. My body responds to him, and I can't control the reactions despite my hatred for him. The moment his lips meet mine, the conflict runs deeper.

His kiss is gentle but claiming all at once. Last night, I had my perfect first kiss, only tainted by the man doing the kissing. I'm beyond innocent with sex and relationships. My father was the *pakhan* of the Saint Petersburg Brotherhood—one of the most powerful brotherhoods Russia had ever seen. He didn't let me go near boys and ruthlessly protected our family.

Andrei's tongue slips into my mouth, tangling with my own. I'm lost, forgetting *who* is kissing me. A shameful moan escapes my lips as the need inside of me increases. I've been so strict with myself even after my family died. I've never once given in to simple pleasure, making it more challenging to keep a handle on my urges.

It all hits me as he bites my lip, making me tense. This man killed my family. I pull away, a conflict raging in my head. So many emotions I can't organize my thoughts amongst the chaos inside of me.

He grabs hold of my hair, fisting it in his hands. "Do you understand what it takes to be submissive?" His dark eyes are burning with pure lust.

I nod my head, averting his gaze.

"Vera, look at me," he commands.

I do, despite wishing I could shy away.

"You won't be in control with me." He tightens his grip on my hair, tugging so it's almost painful. "I will master your body. I will dominate it. You will be mine. Do you understand?" he asks.

"Yes, sir," I say, bowing my head.

He grips hold of my throat in a firm grip, forcing me to meet his gaze. I hate the way I respond to his dominance. My nipples harden, and my core throbs with need. It's enough to make me sick to the stomach.

"Good girl," he says, voice huskier than before. "Get dressed for breakfast."

I swallow hard as he lets go of my throat, thankful he doesn't intend to take me right away. The thought of having him inside of me both excites and disgusts me. I don't understand it, and I can't stand this disgusting lust I have for him.

7

ANDREI

I've been patient the past five days, but every time I kiss or touch Vera, she freezes. It's driving me wild since I'm clawing myself back from taking her the way I want. Vera is the most beautiful woman I've ever met, and I want her to be mine. I must make my mark on her so no other man will *ever* touch her.

After five days together, I wonder if she will ever be at ease with me. Patience is key when dealing with a virgin who has been through hell by her trainers.

Her agreement to be my submissive made me ecstatic, but she's cold toward me—a broken beauty who can't overcome the pain of her past.

Maybe she needs more time. She is a virgin — a woman who can't comprehend what I want and need from her.

From my single previous experience, it takes time.

Jen was the only other virgin who agreed to be my submissive. She wasn't the woman I thought, though. When she tried to go behind my back and leave me for one of my *shestyorka* so publicly, it was dealt with brutally.

If she had come to me and told me the truth, I would have made it happen for her. I wasn't in love with her. We were a good fit in the bedroom, but that was all.

I've longed for a woman I could call my own for a long time, but I'm too cold and cut off. No woman in their right mind would give their heart to me and for a good reason.

It's impossible to love a woman while remaining *pakhan* of such a powerful brotherhood. It's dangerous and doesn't fit.

The door to the dining room opening draws my attention. I can feel my heart rate speed up at the sight of her, almost gliding toward me.

If I were to fall, it would be for her. "Good morning, *Krasivaya*," I say as she sets her hand on the back of the chair next to me at the same time she does every morning.

It's strange the way she is like clockwork, always on time.

She half-smiles, but it doesn't reach her eyes— nothing ever does. "Good morning," she mumbles, sitting down in her chair next to me.

"Did you sleep well?" I ask, remembering the way

she sobbed the first night. Ever since, she hasn't made a sound, to my disappointment.

I've yet to tell her my room adjoins hers. It's why I could hear her that night, and I couldn't lie in my room and do nothing. An unusual need to soothe her had me walking into her room. It has disappointed me that she hasn't given me a reason to go in there again.

"Yes," she says, picking up her fork and cutting into the cold meat on her plate.

My jaw clenches at the short answer, and I focus on my plate. Vera never gives me anything in return, and it's starting to irritate me. There's no attempt from her side to make conversation, no matter how hard I try. As I stew on it, I find my rage growing at how little she offers me.

"Are you sure you wish to be my submissive?" I ask, unable to keep the irritation out of my voice. I sip my orange juice, glancing at her over the rim.

"I am sure, sir. Why do you ask?"

I grab her hand, and she tenses, pulling away. "Because every time I touch you, you flinch."

Her jaw clenches, and there's a flash of something in her eyes. It looks like panic.

"Speak to me, Vera."

She averts her gaze, focusing on her plate and schooling her features. "I will do anything you want." She pauses a moment. "You only need to command me. Isn't that how this works?"

I rub my hand across my neck, trying to keep calm. "Yes, but I expect you to enjoy it." I shake my head. "It's not enjoyable when the woman is not into it."

She nods her head, still not meeting my gaze. "I understand. It's all very new to me," she murmurs.

In an instant, the irritation fades, remembering what she has been through over the past few months alone. God knows what terrors this woman has endured in her life. A virgin is likely to be tense when being touched by a man she doesn't know. I stand from my chair and walk behind hers, touching her shoulders.

A tremble runs from the top of her head down her spine as I knead them. The tension is beyond anything I've felt before. She needs to relax.

"We will start after breakfast," I say.

A tension coils through her shoulders. "Yes, sir," she says, dropping her fork. "I'm finished."

She ate very little, and her appetite has been off since the first night. I push the concern about her eating habits from my mind and let go of her shoulders. "Follow me."

She stands from her chair and walks behind me, keeping her eyes on the ground. No matter what I say, she can't forget her training. I wonder how untouched she is as we walk up the stairs toward my room. She wouldn't have expected this in the morning, but I have no meetings today.

I open the door to my bedroom. It's the first time Vera has been in here. "Inside," I command.

She does as I say, keeping her eyes fixed on the floor. My length is straining against the zipper of my pants. The anticipation of seeing her naked again makes me leak into my tight boxer briefs.

Behind closed doors, I pull my suit jacket off and undo my tie. Vera watches me as I unbutton my shirt, and her eyes dilate when I chuck it off. There's no doubt she's attracted to me.

"Strip," I say, moving my fingers to the buckle of my belt.

She swallows hard and then pulls her t-shirt off, revealing her full breasts to me. Her hard, peaked nipples are pointing in my direction. It takes all the control I have not to rush toward her and suck on them. I groan as I take my pants off, remaining only in my boxers.

She keeps her eyes on the ground as she undoes her pants' button and pushes them down her wide hips. The black lacy underwear she's wearing is sexy as hell. She stops, crossing her arms over her chest.

"Panties off," I say, keeping my voice commanding.

Her cheeks turn an endearing red as she hooks her fingers into the waistband. I watch as she pulls them down her hips, exposing herself to me. The sight has me moving forward. Her cunt is as beautiful as the rest of her. "Lie on my bed on your back."

Her knees wobble as she moves toward the bed. My attention falls on the built-in restraints. The thought of clapping them around her ankles and wrists, forcing her to be at my mercy, is a fantasy I cannot erase from my mind since I set eyes on her. She's lying with her arms crossed over her chest and legs clamped shut.

I move to the top corner of the bed and fix her wrists into the restraints, making sure they are tight. Her eyes widen as she tests them. The darkness inside of me grows as I move to her ankles, longing to keep her thighs parted and open.

She resists as I drag her right ankle apart, fixing it into the leather strap. Next, I move to her left ankle and force it in, too. She doesn't fight this time.

Her entire body is flushed pink, and her cheeks are bright red.

For the first time, a flicker of fear ignites in her eyes, but she has nothing to fear from me. I won't fuck her yet. Although, there's no way she's escaping from me. The darkness inside me builds, memorizing the image of her legs spread wide by the ties at her ankles. I love having a woman at my mercy, knowing she's unable to control what will happen to her or how I'll make her feel. My cock throbs in my tight boxer briefs. I rub my hand over it, groaning. Her pussy is exposed and glistening with arousal.

She watches me with half-fear and half-fascination as I pull my boxers off, freeing my hard length. It slaps back against I walk toward her, teasing the tips of my fingers over her soft, creamy thighs. They quiver at my touch. I kneel between her parted legs and tease a finger through her center. She's soaked—dripping fucking wet.

My mouth waters at the thought of tasting her. "How untouched are you?" I ask, staring into her beautiful, bright green eyes.

She swallows before answering, "Totally untouched, sir."

A low growl rises in my throat. I'll be the first man to lick her, the first man to make her orgasm. I lower my mouth to her arousal and part her lips with my tongue. She whimpers, clawing at the bedsheets as much as the restraints will allow.

I tease her for a short time, nipping and sucking at her outer lips. Once she's quivering, I let my tongue flick over her throbbing clit. She jolts, moaning as I suck it into my mouth. Her pussy floods with even more honeyed nectar, and I lick up every drop.

It is sweeter than honey. This is heaven.

I tease at her lips with two fingers before plunging them inside of her. She's unbelievably tight, and it doesn't help that she's tense. I glance at her, and she's biting her bottom lip, watching me with a conflicted look.

I lick her clit again, watching as her eyes dilate. It won't be long until she gives in to me and the sensations I intend to force her to endure. Her arms pull against the restraints and her legs as I dip my fingers back inside of her.

I break through her careful guards as a deep moan escapes her luscious lips. The dominant side of me rises, rejoicing in the fact I've broken through her walls. It takes all my self-control not to take her now while she's tied and bound for me with her thighs parted.

The need to claim her is clawing at me as I taste her. My tongue plunges inside of her as if I am starving for this woman. I want to consume her — the hunger is growing and taking control of me.

Despite her reserved ways, she lets a high-pitched moan break through the solid barrier she has erected. I let my teeth sink into the skin around her folds, making her moan even more. If there is one thing I know, a small amount of pain always intensifies pleasure as nothing else can.

I let one finger slip inside of her, fingering her deeply while still licking her throbbing clit. Her hips buck toward my face as much as they can, considering she's tied down. I'm only using light restraints. The thought of having her on my bondage bench in my pleasure room makes me want to lose control, but baby steps are best with a virgin.

Her thighs shake as I continue to finger fuck her, slipping a second one inside of her. She moans deeply, clamping her eyes shut. I can't explain how it makes me feel to see her submitting to me.

"Fuck," she moans, trying to claw at the bedsheets beneath her, against the restraints.

I lick and suck on her clit, working my tongue in circles around it. My teeth tease over her arousal. She's dripping wet and leaking all over my fingers.

She mutters something in Russian that I don't quite catch.

I feel her coming undone, her muscles quivering deep inside of her. "Oh my God," she cries out as I fuck her harder with my fingers, forcing her over the edge.

Her cheeks are flushed, and she looks like she's having the first orgasm of her life—maybe she is. The thought makes my balls tingle, but I know I can't immediately push this. "That's it, *Krasivaya*, let me taste every drop of you," I groan, licking her until she's stopped shuddering.

Even though my cock is steel, I shift to lie down next to her, pulling her into my chest. She's like jelly, and her whole body is limp as she rests her head against my chest. Her eyes flicker shut without a word, and I know she's fallen asleep as her breathing deepens.

I'm still hard, but we've got plenty of time to experiment with each other. I can't wait to claim this virgin as my own.

8

VERA

Sickened.

It's the only word that can describe how I feel right now. The guilt of what Andrei did to my body makes me want to puke.

The worst part is that I loved it. Andrei made me feel like I've never felt before. A part of me longed to feel him inside of me. It's as if my body can't fathom the truth my brain is aware of. This man is terrible.

He sleeps by my side, snoozing. I swallow hard as I look at him. The need to end him is overwhelming me.

The razor is in my jeans pocket, and I need to use it now. I can't continue this warped, fucked up thing between us. If we have sex, I won't be able to control my reactions toward him. How could I live with myself if the man who took my virginity was the same man who murdered my family?

I won't have long to live once I kill him, but dying a virgin is better than giving this monster the honor. His brotherhood will slay me for the act. There are worse things in life than dying a virgin, and one of them is screwing a man like him.

I peel the sheets from myself and move toward my pants. The blade is in the back pocket, and I clench it in my fist. The moment the past three years have been leading to. It feels anti-climactic, but maybe nothing would have felt adequate.

I shift back into the bed and flick open the razor. My heart pounds hard in my chest as I gaze at the man, a man who acts differently from how I expected. He's almost kind. As he sleeps, he looks beautiful. I hate the thought, but it's true.

My hand shakes as I position the razor over his throat, ready to cut it open. This moment is one I've foreseen every day for three years, but now, I waver — the blade inches from his throat.

Why can't I do it?

I feel tears of frustration prickle my eyes. Andrei is the first person I've ever attempted to murder, and people told me it isn't easy, no matter how much you detest the person.

It doesn't help that he has shown me kindness since he purchased me.

Where is the evil beast I'd heard so much about?

As I look at him, I can't match him to the cold-blooded murderer of my family.

I shake my head. I've seen the photographs. The images burst into my mind, and I grit my teeth, realizing without a doubt that I've got to kill him. It is now or never.

I'm ready to slice him open as rage courses through my veins. That's when his hand closes around mine, and his eyes shoot open.

I try to force the knife into him, but he's too strong.

Fuck.

Everything I've worked for for the past three years has all ended.

He overpowers me, chucking the razor onto the floor out of reach. There is a frantic rage in his eyes as he forces me beneath him and pins me to the bed. His cock is hard against my tummy, throbbing.

"What the fuck are you doing, Vera?" he growls, searching my eyes.

I claw onto my shield, the only thing I have left, despite the urge to scream and shout the truth at him. The essential rule my uncle taught me was never to let your guard down. I bite my lip, glaring at him.

"Answer me," he growls.

I turn my head away.

"Why were you trying to kill me?" There's a controlled and dangerous fury in his voice.

He doesn't scare me. He can kill me for all I care. The aim was to get revenge, and I've failed. My life is pointless. Uncle will never forgive me for this.

I gasp as his mouth clashes with mine, kissing me hard and deep. I resist trying to stop him. His tongue slips into my mouth, and I bite down on it, but not hard enough to dissuade him.

He groans against my mouth, biting my lip in return and drawing blood.

We remain tangled in a battle of lust and hate, warring against each other with our tongues and lips. The longer he persists, the more my body betrays me.

I claw at the man I tried to kill a few moments ago, kissing him with a broken and sick fury. My mind knows this is wrong, but my body doesn't care.

He finds my center and slips two thick fingers into my soaking wet heat. I cry out at the sudden invasion as he kisses my neck and throat, biting my collarbone hard enough to leave his mark. His eyes are wild and frantic.

I should be dead. Andrei should kill me for trying to end his life—a *pakhan*'s life. Instead, he's kissing me and touching me. I moan against his mouth, biting down on his lip enough to draw blood and taste it in my mouth.

He growls and then teases my clit, sending me rushing toward the edge of the explosion. He holds me down with one hand and grabs something from his bedside cabinet.

My eyes widen when I see him holding up a ball gag. He forces it into my mouth and tightens it around the back of my head. "No more biting," he groans, grinding his long, thick length into me.

There's such conflict inside of me. It feels like I'm being torn in two. My body reacts to his ministrations in a way I despise and love at the same time. I'm at his mercy, restrained by his sheer power and size.

He grabs hold of my wrists, slapping the restraints on tighter than before. He does the same to my ankles, holding me down to the bed without mercy. His cock is free from his boxers within seconds, and he rubs the thick, swollen head through my center, coating himself in my juices.

Fear, panic, and wanton desire flood me all at once.

Is he going to take me?

The man I loathe is about to fuck me without my permission. He doesn't need my permission, as he owns me. I'm his virgin to do with what he wants. I brace myself, clamping my eyes shut and waiting.

Instead, he returns to his haunches and lowers his mouth to me. I writhe in pure ecstasy as he kisses me there with such tenderness compared to how he kissed me. There is such conflicting intensity in how he devours me — one minute hot and furious, the next controlled and careful.

My mind turns to a blank mess when he slips his fingers inside of me, hooking them inside of me. The pressure is building, and it is a hot, fiery need that takes over my body. My mind no longer fights to hold on to the truth. No matter how hard I try to cling to my resolve and force myself to hate it, I can't.

I moan around the ball gag in my mouth the moment his tongue connects with the sensitive nerves between my thighs, sending unmatched pleasure through my body.

The tightness of the leather restraints cut into my skin, adding a thrilling pain. He drags his teeth across my clit, and I could explode. He halts, making me whimper.

"I won't let you come until you tell me why you tried to kill me," he says, eyes meeting mine. There's darkness burning in his irises, and he isn't bluffing.

I swallow hard, recalling my training. Admittedly, being submitted to torturous pleasure and no release will be no different from withstanding pain with no release. I shut my eyes and try to picture the place I always go to.

A hard hand slams into my thighs, forcing my eyes open.

"Keep your eyes open," he growls.

He slaps me again on the other thigh. I moan, finding the pain thrilling. It's not what I'm used to—pain isn't pleasurable. This is different when he slaps me, and it lights me up.

I try to breathe as he works on my clit again, sucking and nipping me with his teeth. My body is wound so tightly. The release is the only thing I crave now, but he won't give it to me.

He knows my body better than I do. Every time I'm seconds from coming undone, he holds me there and denies me the pleasure.

He stops and gazes at me. "Are you ready to tell me yet?"

I shake my head, glaring at him. No one broke me in that bastard virgin camp, and he won't be the one to do it.

He continues to torture me, drawing out my pleasure. The need for release is challenging to resist, but I won't break. Pain is easy to block out after enduring so much training to be ready for it. No training prepared me for what this man is subjecting me to.

I can't tell you how long he continued because it felt like a lifetime. Every time, he pushes me to the edge, only to back off at the last second.

His ability to read the way my body works is impressive. By the time he gives up, tears prickle my eyes, and I can't breathe.

He moves to undo the restraints from my ankles, still not offering me my release. I clamp my thighs shut, feeling embarrassed and violated. He sits back on his haunches. His huge cock is still semi-hard. "Vera, look at me," he commands.

Out of instinct, I do as he says, looking into his dark brown eyes.

"Whatever revenge you want against me is most likely the result of lies." He narrows his eyes. "Many men want me dead, but I can't think of a reason a girl like you would want me dead."

Bastard.

He killed them. I saw the photos of him with the knife and the blood dripping from it. He stood over their bodies and watched them die.

I feel my throat constricting as he shifts forward to undo the gag, allowing me to draw breath. As he frees me from them, a sudden flood of pent-up emotions hit me.

I bite my lip, trying to keep the truth inside, holding on with as much restraint as I can, even though he has caught me in the act.

What difference does it make now?

"You killed them," I wail, feeling a mix of rage, sadness, and odd release bubbling inside of me. The tears threaten to spill down my cheeks.

He kneels before me, still naked. This situation is so fucked up. "I killed who?"

"My family," I say, tears falling down my cheeks as I remember the moment I found them as if only yesterday. The pain is so acute, as I never mourned them—not properly.

"When?" he asks. His eyes are hard as steel, and his jaw clenches.

"Three years ago, in Saint Petersburg."

He grabs my hand and squeezes. "That would be rather difficult, considering I haven't returned to Russia for ten years since I fled with my father."

The restraints on my wrists make it impossible to get away from him. "You're a liar," I spit.

He stands, walking to the other side of the room. When he returns, he's holding his passport. "I haven't been out of America for ten years." He holds the passport up and flicks through it. "Whoever told you this lied." I shake my head, unable to process what he's saying. He must have left with a different passport. "I saw the photos of you standing over my family."

He brushes a hair from my face and tucks it behind my ear in a far too gentle gesture. "I didn't do it, Vera." I watch him as he thinks for a moment. "Someone probably used photo manipulation. Who was your family?"

I narrow my eyes at him, but a nagging doubt forms. Is Andrei telling the truth? His character isn't what my uncle described. He learned I'm here to kill him, and he's acting with kindness and understanding.

"My father was Ivan Popov," I say, my voice quiet.

He tenses and stares at me with wide eyes. "The Ivan Popov? The infamous *pakhan* of the Saint Petersburg brotherhood?"

I nod my head. "Yes."

He blows out a long breath. "I never met your father or the rest of your family." The sincerity in his eyes makes me question everything I've believed. "I mourned for him when I heard of his passing. Everyone here did. My father knew him well."

I say nothing. I can't. The lump in my throat makes it impossible to speak. As I try to process what Andrei tells me, my world is falling apart. My uncle insisted Andrei killed them before fleeing back to America.

He showed me the images—but what if Andrei is right? Igor could have manipulated me with photoshopped photos.

My uncle told me if I didn't kill him within a week of the auction, he would come and do the job himself.

Andrei presses his hand to my cheek. "How can I prove this to you?" he asks, searching my eyes for the answer.

There are no words I can find to reply to him. I sit stunned, confused, and more broken than ever. The only thing holding me together was my quest for revenge, and now that is gone.

If Andrei didn't kill my parents and siblings, then who did?

9

ANDREI

I'm numb. I've been sitting in my office for six hours, trying to focus on the proposals Alexi asked me to review, but I can't concentrate.

Vera Popov tried to kill me. Vera Popov was assumed dead with the rest of her family, but her body was never found. My father had known Ivan well when he was in Russia. They were good friends a long time ago. Although I never got the chance to meet him, the stories my father told me of him made me sure he was a good man.

The culprit of her family's murder was never found, so whoever was behind it tried to use her to get to me. They intended to pin the murder on me to get rid of me. It's all I can think about, coupled with the beautiful woman locked in her bedroom. Vera is waiting for me to punish her.

I should kill her. An eye for an eye is the Bratva way.

I don't want to. A deep and primal connection inside of me that makes it impossible to consider harming Vera. All I want to do is claim her as my own.

Someone told her I killed her family, which couldn't be further from the truth. When my father heard about the death of Ivan Popov and his family in Saint Petersburg, the entire brotherhood mourned them.

It's believed that his merciful ways were the reason for his death. In the Bratva, mercy is a weakness and is exploited. Someone has manipulated her to believe a lie — an attempt from Russia to end me once and for all.

I let my tongue flick out over the cut on my lip, where Vera bit me. I feel so desperate to take her. I was close to getting on with it, thrusting inside of her and claiming her as my own.

The need for her is twisted and fucked up since she tried to kill me. A dark part of me wants to make her mine and put a baby inside of her so no other man will ever go near her.

It makes little sense, considering. I can't bring a woman like her into my life. Danger follows me everywhere I go, and life is easier for me if I have no attachments.

Since we fled ten years ago, people in the brotherhood have been after my father and me. They hated how powerful we'd become over here. They hated that we stole from them—but that's not what happened. They framed my father ten years ago, and now I've been framed for a murder I couldn't have committed.

A knock at the door breaks me from my thoughts. Alexi pops his head through the door. "Sir, Lyov is here to see you."

I narrow my eyes at him. "What does he want?" Lyov is one of our spies who oversees our operations on the ground, reporting to me. He rarely comes to me without a prearranged appointment.

He shrugs. "He didn't say."

My brow furrows, but I nod my head. "Fine, bring him in."

Alexi leaves to fetch him, and I wonder what is so crucial that Lyov came here without even a call ahead. I tap my fingers against the wood of my desk, waiting.

Lyov enters the room, and he looks as severe as ever. He's a harsh guy who hasn't come to terms with the American culture. I've never seen him smile, not once, not even with the brothers in our brotherhood.

"Lyov, to what do I owe this unannounced pleasure?"

If he's worried about showing up to his *pakhan's* office without an appointment, he doesn't show it, which is surprising considering what I did to Petrov last week.

During an urgent meeting with our arms dealers, he interrupted me, and I threw him out of the brotherhood after a rather brutal beating. Lyov may be a higher rank than him, but sometimes he's too cocky for his good. As *pakhan*, I have to keep him in check.

He crosses his arms over his chest and stares at me. "There's a rumor of an attempt on your life, sir."

I wave my hand in the air. "What's new?"

He shakes his head, eyes serious. "It's believed they compromised the virgin you purchased at the auction."

The pounding of my heart thuds in my ears, but I don't let him know I'm affected by his claim. "Are you suggesting that a young woman can get the better of me?" I ask, standing to my feet.

Lyov is a good spy, but he can often overstep the mark when speaking to me. As *pakhan*, he shouldn't insult me with such an insinuation.

"No, sir." He bows his head. "I wished to inform you of her training."

I step forward and stand in front of him. "How did you learn of this?"

He meets my gaze. "I received word from Russia."

I grit my teeth. "Thank you, Lyov." My eyes narrow as he doesn't make a move to leave. "Is there anything else?"

He averts his gaze, clearing his throat. "Yes, there are reports of the Miami Brotherhood making a play in our territory again." He rubs his hand across the back of his neck. "They are becoming increasingly aggressive, and it is only a matter of time until we have to take action."

I step toward the dresser in my office, pouring myself a glass of bourbon. The Miami brotherhood of the Bratva has been overstepping for the past six months. It's something I should have discussed with Luka at the auction, but I was too distracted by my purchase.

The warm, woody whiskey heats my throat and chest as it goes down. "What kind of action would you propose?" I don't turn to face him, keeping my back to my spy.

"A kidnapping might be the quickest show of power," Lyov says.

My jaw clenches at the prospect. "Very well, keep a tab on Luka's actions. If it gets worse, then bring forward a proposal."

There are a few beats of silence before he replies, "Sir."

I turn to see him bow his head and leave the room. Kidnapping is a foul way to get what you want, but unfortunately, it is most often the best way to reduce life loss. One innocent person has to suffer to save many lives.

I crack my neck, feeling the tension coiling

through my muscles. Lyov believes I'm Vera is a threat —a young woman who has lost everything. He may be right. I'm in danger of losing something, but I know it's not my life.

She's confused and lost, and deep down, I long to help her find her way. Maybe we could be lost together — two broken and wounded souls, finding each other. I shake my head, knowing my thoughts are certifiably insane.

Vera tried to kill me. All I should be considering is how I will take her life. I stand from my chair, scooting around my desk. There's no way I can stay in this cramped, confined office a moment longer. I walk straight out of my office and up the stairs.

I know that pursuing Vera is a bad idea. Going near that girl ever again is a bad idea, but the thought of never talking to her and shipping her away riles me. It's worse than thinking about what might happen if she's successful in her assassination attempt.

As I climb the stairs toward her room, I realize how insane that is. I'd rather die than see her hurt or harmed or even taken from me. Her bedroom is silent. I wait outside the door, my heart pounding fast. My stomach twists with anxiety at the prospect of seeing her.

What am I supposed to say to her?

I reach for the doorknob, twisting it and pausing a moment. When I swing open the door, my eyes land on Vera. She's fast asleep on top of the covers of the bed. A strange giddiness comes over me when I see her. The fact she tried to kill me hasn't dulled the need to claim her as my own.

She may be mine since I purchased her, but it's not what I want. I want her to give herself over to me, even if she hates me at the moment.

A mumble from the bed has me starting forward, noticing she's waking up. Her eyes flick open, and she stares at me, taking my breath from my lungs. Those emerald eyes cut me every time.

"I came to check on you," I say, lingering a few feet away from her.

She shifts in the bed, backing toward the headboard. "Are you going to kill me now?"

I shake my head, irritated that she would ask me that question. There's nothing that could force me to harm her. She's an angel, my angel. "No." I slip my hands into my pockets and move to sit on the edge of the bed.

She looks down at the bedsheets, twisting them between her fingers.

"I don't intend to hurt you ever."

Her eyes shoot back up, and she stares at me in disbelief. "I tried to kill you."

She watches as I shift closer, reaching to touch her face. A muscle clenches in her jaw, but she doesn't move away from me, not this time. "Someone has manipulated you, Printsessa."

Vera sinks her teeth into her bottom lip, searching

my eyes for the truth. I grab her hand, squeezing. "I promise I will discover what happened to your mother, father, brother, and sister."

A flash of pain ignites before she blocks it out. "Why?" she croaks out, averting my gaze.

"My father was good friends with your father, Ivan Popov. He mourned his death." I shrug. "I may not have known him, but he was a friend of my father. If my father were here, he would want me to help you."

I shift on the bed even closer to her, longing to touch her. The memory of the way I made her writhe and beg for release on this same bed makes me ache to be inside of her.

She watches me but doesn't shy away. I let my hand slip behind her neck, gripping possessively. Her lips part, and her eyes dilate as I move toward hers.

I tease my lips against hers, enjoying how she draws breath into her lungs in surprise. The sound is hardly audible but enough to stir more need. I tighten my grip around the back of her neck and pull her hard against me, deepening the kiss.

There's something savage and desperate about the way she makes me feel. My tongue teases against her lips, demanding entrance. For a second, it appears she won't submit. When she does, my cock thickens in my pants.

Vera moans into my mouth, letting her hand fall to my thigh. She digs her fingers in and tries to pull away from me.

"What's wrong?" I ask.

"Everything." She shakes her head. "I don't know what to believe."

"Believe me, Vera," I breathe.

Her tongue flicks out over her lips, drawing my eyes to them again. This time, she moves forward, pressing her soft, plump lips to mine in an innocent kiss. I long to take her and make her mine. The not-so-sweet virgin who tried to kill me. It may not make any sense, but life never does.

I may see some of myself in her. A girl who has been warped and manipulated into becoming something she wouldn't be in another life.

If someone sent her here to kill me, it means I'm no longer safe in New York for now. Lyov knew that. I plan to move somewhere else, and Vera will come with me.

10

VERA

*T*he ropes graze against the sore skin on my wrists as I sit frozen in the car seat. I won't tell him how much he has derailed me or how scared I am. Andrei can't see that he has affected me with his claim.

I can smell him close — his strong pine and musk scent encasing me in the back of the moving vehicle. The roar of the engine is the only sound that falls between us.

I flinch as a hand connects with my thigh, squeezing. Andrei's touch is more confusing than anything else. He's gentle but dominating. A quality I find so intoxicating despite everything.

The hood over my head blocks all light as I try to move away. The panic I feel at being in total darkness is high. Andrei doesn't know how much I hate the dark, but it's putting me on edge.

"*Rasslabsia,*" he mutters in a soft, husky voice. Relax in Russian.

The tone only reminds me of what he did to me yesterday morning. I can't stop thinking about the way he made me feel. The phantom touch of his lips on mine, his teeth sinking into my lip, and the pain that only intensified the pleasure he ignited deep inside me.

"Where are we going?" I ask, recognizing my only voice.

The hand on my thigh tightens. "You will see."

I tense at the dark tone of his voice. Three years of discipline and control training to ensure I never found myself in this exact situation. I'm no longer in the driver's seat.

Andrei's promise keeps repeating in my mind. It is like a broken record, playing repeatedly.

I will discover what happened to your mother, father, brother, and sister. I promise.

The way he kissed me only confused me more. I've never felt this way. How can I want a man who I spent years hating?

It feels like we're driving for ages, the darkness making it easy to fall in and out of troubled sleep. Finally, the vehicle comes to a stop. Andrei shifts next to me and whisks the hood off of my head. I'm surprised to see it's already pitch-black outside.

It's impossible to tell where we are, but from the moon's reflection in a glass-like substance to the left, I assume we're near water — a flood of panic coils through me from head to toe.

Andrei may intend to torture me or kill me. Even though, after the way he's acted toward me, I'm sure that's unlikely, the worry is always there.

Water is one of my biggest fears since the day my family died. I found them floating on the edge of the stream that ran through our garden, blood staining it a deep red.

Ever since I have gone nowhere near water, the fear of being close to it again paralyzes me. Andrei gets out of the car, slamming the door shut.

I remain still and unmoving, staring at the shimmering liquid lit by the stars and moon in the night sky.

He comes to my side and opens the door, pulling me out and into his arms. I shiver as he stares at me.

"I'm sorry about the ropes." He glances at my wrists. "My *sovietnik* insisted I take precautions, but now it's just us. I'll take them off once we're inside." He nods toward the log cabin we've pulled up outside. I was too focused on the water to notice it.

His warm, hard body remains pressed against me as he carries me toward the home, lifting me over the threshold as one of his men opens the door for us. Once inside, he sets me down on my feet.

"Is there anything else, sir?" His man asks.

Andrei shakes his head. "No, that will be all. Thank you, Yakov."

He gives me a wary look, glancing between his boss and me again, before bowing his head and leaving us alone. I can't understand why my thighs quiver at that thought. I'm alone with him.

He starts toward me, and I take a step back as he draws a knife. My heart rate pounds, and I try to run for it, tripping over a step behind me. "Vera, I've told you I won't hurt you." His firm but gentle grip lands on my arm, and he uses the knife to cut the ropes around my wrists. "I want you to trust me."

I rub my red, rope-burned skin, glancing at him. "Sorry." I shake my head. "It's hard for me to trust anyone." I glance around the stylish and well-decorated log cabin, feeling the heat of the roaring fire. "Where are we?"

Andrei steps toward me. "My safe house." His arms wrap around my shoulders, and he guides me toward the living area, nearer to the fire. "My men are working to find out who killed your family."

A twinge of pain ignites in my chest, making it difficult to breathe. "We're no longer in the New York area?"

His dark eyes flash, and he shakes his head. "Sit."

I do as he says, sinking into the plush, beige sofa in front of the fire.

He sits beside me, setting a hand on my thigh. "We will stay here as long as necessary, Printsessa." He shifts closer to me, staring at me with such intensity I can feel my panties dampening by the second.

Ever since he has touched me in that way, I can no longer ignore the sick craving for him deep inside of me.

It still makes me feel ashamed that I want him. Even though I'm sure he didn't kill my family, he's a man I've spent three years hating. I've spent three years plotting his murder, for God's sake.

"I still want you to be my submissive, Vera," he says, voice laced with hot desire.

I lick my bottom lip, wanting to give it all to him despite everything. He grabs my chin, tilting my face toward him. "You are so damn beautiful." He moves his lips closer to mine.

I shut my eyes as he kisses me—somehow, it makes it more bearable. Part of me wants this more than anything, but another part is programmed to believe he is the enemy. It feels like I'm being torn in two.

He senses my reluctance and moves away. "What's wrong?"

"I-I don't know… I can't believe how wrong I got everything."

He nods and stands, walking away from the sofa and into the kitchen. "I will get dinner started, and then we can talk."

I blink twice, watching as he grabs a pan out of the cupboard. If there's one thing I never expected to see Andrei Petrov do, it is cook for me.

He opens the fridge door and pulls out the ingredients. "Do you like *Blinis*?"

I stand and walk toward him, wondering how this man is the same one who I'd heard all these awful stories of. "Yes, I love them." I didn't mention that my dad used to cook them for us when we were kids. The thought of Andrei cooking them for me now makes my stomach flutter with nerves.

"I've got mincemeat or cheese for the filling. Which do you prefer?"

I sink my teeth into my bottom lip. "Mincemeat filling and cheese on top," I say, remembering how I loved them when my dad did them like that.

He smiles at me. "Exactly how I like them."

I watch as he gets to work, finding it soothing to see him cooking for me. It also means he can't touch me either, as he's too busy. I'm afraid of what I will do alone with him.

After we've both finished eating, I stand and clear the plates. Andrei's chair scrapes across the ground, alerting me that he is following me. I set the dishes in the sink and turn on the water, waiting for it to get hot.

His presence behind me is impossible to ignore as warmth permeates the surrounding air. That pine, masculine scent invades my senses, making me weak at the knees.

"Vera," he utters my name so softly it sets the hair on the back of my neck. His arms go around me from behind, and he pins me against the counter, the weight of him solid but warm.

The thick, throbbing length of him presses against my ass. I reach for the detergent, but he stops me, moving my hands to the taps and forcing me to turn them off. "The dishes can wait," he murmurs in my ear.

I shiver in anticipation. There's no doubt that I'm at threat of sleeping with this man. Andrei is a man I hated for so long despite never meeting him.

He moves my hair to one side and kisses my shoulder and neck gently. I moan as his hands stroke my thighs, traveling beneath my dress. His fingers are edging closer and closer to my dripping wet pussy. He rubs my clit through my lace panties. "You're so fucking wet, Printsessa."

I arch my back as his fingers dip inside of me. The sensations he gives me flood me with conflicting emotions and feelings.

"Fuck," I say, finally giving in to this warped attraction.

"That's it, Vera," he groans, grinding his cock against my ass. The only thing between us is his clothes. "Submit to me," he growls, nipping my ear and sending an electrifying pain through my body.

I'm lost. The woman I was when Andrei bought me is gone. I don't know who I am anymore. I don't know what I want anymore.

How can everything I believed unravel so quickly?

He digs his fingertips into my hips and spins me around quickly, making me gasp. Our eyes meet, and his burn with such hunger makes me moan. "Do you still want to be my submissive, Vera?"

I nod my head, unable to find the words. This man is impossible to resist. His dominance calls to a part of myself I thought I'd buried three years ago. A part of me longs to live and give in to my needs and wants. When my family died, I gave up on living.

"Answer me," he says, eyes flashing.

"Yes, I want you to take me, sir," I say, my voice so quiet and laced with desire I can barely recognize it.

His lips descend on mine frantically, and he lifts me into his arms. I hook my own around his neck, and he carries me out of the living area. He kicks open the door to a large, plush bedroom.

I swallow hard as he sets me down in the center of the bed, noticing the restraints already fitted to each corner.

How many women has he made submit to him on this bed?

I can't understand why an odd sense of jealousy rises in me, contemplating it. Andrei hasn't even fucked me yet, and I can't stand thinking about him touching another woman.

I watch as he slips out of his tailored suit jacket, casting it aside. He then unbuttons his shirt, revealing his perfect, sculpted muscles — my mouth waters. Andrei is pure male perfection.

"Undress," he says as his fingers tease at his belt.

I scramble to unzip my dress at the side, pushing it off and revealing my breasts to him.

He groans, grabbing his hard cock in his boxer briefs. The sight of him like that makes me moan. I need this man inside of me. It may be ridiculous. It may make no sense, but it's all I need.

"Take me," I say, letting my fingers drop between my thighs.

"Off," he commands.

I hook my finger into the waistband of my panties and pull them down, revealing myself to him.

"Perfect," he says.

I lick my lips as he grabs the waistband of his boxers and shifts them down his muscled hips. The thought of seeing him naked again makes me even wetter. The last time, I was torn, but this time, I want him. I watch as he pulls them down, and his cock springs free, slapping against his abs.

The size of him is almost impossible to register. Somehow, it looks bigger than the first time I saw it — the thick head beading with pearly liquid.

He walks to one side of the bed. "Lie down with your head over the side."

I do as he says, eager to please him. The tip of his cock is inches from my lips. I know what he wants from me, and my pussy aches at the thought of sucking him. Any part of him inside of me excites me beyond comprehension.

"Open wide, *Krasivaya.*"

I open my mouth, accepting the hot, throbbing head of his cock inside. He groans the moment my tongue touches him, tasting the salty liquid dripping from the tip. "Relax your throat and breathe through your nose. If you need me to stop, grab my hand," he instructs.

I do as he says as every hot, thick inch of him slides down my throat. It's impossible to breathe any other way than through my nose. The thickness of him pushes against the back of my throat, spilling his salty pre-cum down it. I panic, gagging on him and spilling saliva all over my face and his cock.

He pulls back, "*Rasslabsia,* breathe through your nose."

I nod my head, and he slides in. The throbbing heat of him there makes me wetter than I've ever been as he fucks my throat gently. I focus on breathing through my nose and gagging less. It's impossible to fit every inch of him into my throat.

I hum around his cock, letting him take total control. The lack of control is freeing as he gropes my breasts in his rough hands, using me the way he wants. Saliva drips all over his cock and my face, and tears prickle in my eyes.

"Fuck, Vera," he groans, increasing the tempo.

More drops of his salty, masculine liquid slide down my throat. It's a flavor that drives me wild—his taste. I'm suddenly filled with a wanton need to swallow every drop of his seed.

He keeps fucking my throat while cupping my

breasts in his hands. My hard nipples ache at his touch.

To my annoyance, he pulls out of my throat, panting. "What are you doing?"

He shakes his head and grabs my hair, forcing me to sit upright. "I'm in control, Vera. No questions."

He grabs hold of my hips, flipping me over and forcing me onto my hands and knees. It's as if he's an animal, as he feasts on my pussy with a frantic need. Within seconds, I'm panting and struggling to catch my breath. The hot, fiery pleasure building faster than I've ever known.

His hand comes down hard on my left ass cheek three times before switching to my right for three spanks. I come undone on the last erotic stroke of his hand, unable to hold on any longer.

My whole body is shaking with the force of an orgasm that makes me dizzy and breathless. I can't see as he keeps on licking and sucking at me, kneading the sore skin on my backside.

I try to get out of his hard, firm grip. The need to gain some control of the situation makes it impossible to stay still. "Don't fight it, Vera." He slaps my ass again, hard enough to sting. "Let me dominate you."

Dominate.

I feel every muscle in my body tremble at the word. All my life, I've been in control. Andrei wants me to submit that control, which turns me on and scares me simultaneously.

"You will feel so good if you let me take control," he groans against my arousal, licking me. "Give in to me, Vera." His voice is husky and low.

It breaks the last of my resistance as I let him take control. It's freeing and arousing as I stop struggling in his grip. His tongue returns to my center, dipping inside of me.

I moan, clawing my fingers into the expensive bedding. Andrei licks my clit and then dips his fingers inside of me. The sudden invasion sends a burst of hot pressure through me.

I've just had an orgasm, but another is building quickly. The way he reads my body is like a book. "Andrei," I mutter his name, trying to hold on.

"Come for me, *Krasivaya*." He slaps my ass hard three times on each check.

I scream his name as he sends me over the edge, my body convulsing. For a moment, I can't hear or see. It's as if my brain has short-circuited.

Maybe I died from too much pleasure. As I come to my senses, I'm on my back. Andrei is looming over me, and my hands are tightly bound in the restraints.

His cock is resting against my dripping-wet entrance. The look in his eyes is unadulterated hunger. I know what is about to happen. The man I was sent here to kill is about to take my virginity.

11

ANDREI

*V*era stares at me with flushed cheeks and dilated pupils, surrounded by that stunning emerald hue of her eyes. I'm desperate to fuck her, but I need to make her come at least once more. She's a virgin, and the more I make her come, the better it will be for her.

I lower my mouth to her center, breathing over her sensitive clit. She whimpers, pulling at the restraints. Her eyes are wild and frantic. Ever since I saw her, I've wanted to claim her as my own. Dominate her body in every way possible and make sure she never finds a man who can make her feel the way I do.

I lick a path through her slick, wet folds.

She digs her fingers into the bedsheets, trying to find something to hold on to.

My tongue teases at her perfect asshole, making

her gasp in shock. The tension that coils through her easing the moment I probe at it again. "Fuck," she mutters, eyes wide.

"Do you like that, Printsessa?" I lick her there again, letting my tongue shift deeper into her forbidden back hole. "Do you like me licking your asshole?"

She nods her head. "Yes, sir."

"Good girl," I groan against her, moving from that forbidden place to lick her sweet-as-hell juices again.

She bucks her hips, trying to gain control. Little does she know that she has no control over me. I will make her submit. She will be mine.

I drag the tip of my tongue through her lips, working my way to that sensitive nub. She makes the most delicious sound as I circle the tip of my tongue around her clit. It is like music to my ears. She's so fucking wet.

My cock is aching and hard between my thighs. When I fucked Vera's throat, it took all my self-control not to explode down it. I have to have control all the time, even if Vera makes me teeter on the edge of losing my mind.

She's gorgeous, perfect, everything I've ever wanted in a submissive. Although she's new to every-thing, this is her calling. She's a natural submissive. I let my teeth sink into her clit.

"Andrei," she cries out my name, writhing beneath me. "Fuck."

I dip three fingers into her right to the knuckle, feeling the fluttering of her muscles. She's about to come. I've never been with a woman I can bring to climax so quickly in my life. She's so untouched and so fucking innocent.

I fist my cock in my hands, the desperate need to be inside of her building and increasing deep within me. It makes little sense why I'm so out of control. Normally, I can hold off for far longer than this.

I sink my teeth into her thigh enough to leave a mark. She gasps, and then I suck on her clit, sending her right over the edge.

Her body convulses and pulses with pleasure. A flood of sweet nectar drips from her, and I shift to lap up every drop. I lick her for ages, making sure I don't waste any.

Once she has finally come down to earth, I move to kneel between her legs and rub the head of my aching cock between her lips.

She gazes up at me with a dazed look. Her lips parted, and her cheeks red. I groan at the sight of her hard nipples peaked toward me and lower my mouth to them, sucking on each one for a short while.

The noises she makes are so satisfying. My cock is dripping all over her pussy, making it messy with my seed. I want to mark her, breed her even. It's oddly fucked up. "I will make you mine, Vera," I breathe against her lips before kissing her hard. My tongue tangles with hers, sucking on it.

I sit back on my haunches and grab my cock, rubbing the thick, throbbing head through her lips. She cries out as I grind my cock through her center, bumping it over her clit with each thrust.

"Andrei," she moans my name, making me wild with untamed passion.

I grab her throat and force her eyes to mine.

She swallows thickly, and I can feel the movement beneath my fingers.

Both of us want and need this. It feels like I won't be right again until I'm inside Vera. I use my free hand to guide the tip of my cock to her entrance and push gently. She's so wet and relaxed that my cock slides inside of her easily.

A gasp turns into a moan as I slide inch after inch as deep as I can go. I groan at the tightness of Vera's pussy, squeezing my length so fucking perfectly. "Tebe eto nravitsya?" I wrap my hand around her throat, asking if she likes it in Russian.

"Yes, sir," she moans, understanding my Russian with no trouble. She is, after all, from Saint Petersburg.

I grunt as I slide the last inch inside of her, loving the way it feels to be balls deep — her lips part as she gazes at me. "Mine," I growl, capturing those full lips with my own and pushing my tongue deep inside her mouth.

My body longs to be connected to her as fully as possible. I pull my hips back before slamming into her again, hard and fast — the need to dominate her body ruling me.

"Bistreye," she cries out.

I grunt, fucking her faster, as per her request in Russia, despite wanting to shoot my seed deep inside her tight pussy already. It's the first I've heard her speak Russian, and it's sexy as hell.

My cock leaks inside of her as I grit my teeth and fuck her harder and faster. The slap of skin meeting skin echoes around the cabin bedroom. I withdraw my cock from her heat, reaching over to undo the restraints around her wrists.

I lift her, forcing her onto her knees. I slap her perfect, firm ass.

She bucks her hips, attempting to get my cock inside of her as I rub the tip through her.

"You are so fucking perfect," I groan, sliding my cock back inside of her. I slap her ass as I pound into her.

The noises she is making are pure ecstasy. The moment I set eyes on her, this is what I wanted. To claim her and make her *mine*. To make her feel so good. This beautiful virgin was untouched until I got my hands on her.

My balls ache as I keep fucking her hard and fast, leaking deep inside of her. A need to breed, making me crazy. The only other time I slept with one of my virgins, I made sure she was on birth control before I fucked her.

The virgins are never on it while being trained. Vera is unprotected, but somehow, it makes this even more exciting. Her ass is red with the welts I've given her—my *mark* on her. I growl as I try to keep control. She has to come on my cock.

I need to feel her pussy fluttering around me as I tip her over the edge for the fourth time this evening.

"Harder," she moans, making my balls clench.

"Fuck, baby," I groan, gritting my teeth and fucking her even harder.

She loves it rough, and it's so fucking hot. I grab her throat from behind, choking her as I pound my cock in and out of her tight heat. "You are so fucking tight."

Her pussy tightens around me, and she floods with her honeyed nectar, making my mouth water.

"Andrei," she cries out my name as she comes undone. Her body is convulsing as I keep my hand firm around her throat. I lean forward and suck on her ear lobe, pounding her two more times before I explode.

I roar as my balls empty as deep as I can go inside of her. I won't stop until I'm certain every drop of my seed is inside of her as deep as possible.

She has gone limp, and I shift my arms to her waist and lift her while I'm still inside of her. Sitting down on the bed, I hold her in my arms, keeping my still-hard cock deep within her. I don't care if we make a mess. This moment is perfect as I kiss her softly and lazily, making this moment last as long as possible.

It's official. Vera is mine.

Vera stands by the lake's edge, hugging her thick shawl around her shoulders. It's a beautiful view. A stunning woman is standing in front of this stunning nature. If I had a camera, I'd take a picture to remember this moment forever.

I open the cabin door and walk toward her, cursing my shoes that clack on the wooden decking. She glances back at me, and I can tell she's been crying.

The tough assassin who came to kill me is opening up her heart. "Good morning, Printsessa," I say, shifting to stand by her side.

"Good morning." She returns her attention to the water, eyes puffy and red.

"Are you okay?"

She hugs herself even tighter, shaking her head. "I haven't been near the water since…"

I step by her side and rest a hand on her shoulder, forcing her to look at me. "Since their death?"

She nods, averting my gaze and looking over the water. "Yes."

I watch her in fascination, wondering how such a beautiful creature was created. My arm slides around her waist, and I pull her close. She lets me hold her, and it makes a nice difference.

Vera rests her hand chest, leaning into me. After taking her virginity last night, I know how deep I am in this. The woman who tried to kill me is infecting my heart. A cold, barren wasteland that hasn't let anyone in since my father's death.

We connected on a level I've never experienced before. It was beautiful and natural, as if we were made for each other.

The sound of a gunshot startles both of us, and my first instinct is to push Vera behind me, blocking her with my body. Another one rings out, and this time, blood paints the decking of the log cabin. The adrenaline makes it impossible to feel the pain. I glance down and find blood spilling from my shoulder.

"Quick, inside," I shout, grabbing her and pushing her toward the cabin.

She dashes inside, turning to me when the door is shut and locked. "You're hit," she says, rushing toward me.

"It's a flesh wound, don't worry." I nod toward the sofas. "Get down behind them." She gives me a reluctant glance. "Now." She rushes to crouch behind the furniture.

I narrow my eyes and scan the front of the house through the bulletproof glass front. Whoever shot me is staying hidden. I duck as a bullet hits the glass, cracking it.

We're under attack, and I've only got a few men nearby. If they made it to the cabin, it means they got through them. I keep my head down and duck behind the sofa, joining Vera. "They've got us surrounded."

Her eyes are wide. "What are we going to do?"

I kiss her, knowing this could all go south. "I want you to stay down and hidden, no matter what. Do you understand?"

Her eyes are defiant as she glares at me. "No, I won't stand by and do nothing while you fight."

I grab hold of her shoulders and dig my fingers in. "Vera, do as I say. I won't see you hurt."

Her gaze softens, and she nods her head. I'm not convinced that she will stay hidden, but it's all I can do right now.

I stand from our hiding place, drawing my gun from my belt and screwing on my silencer. The cabin has too many windows, but they are bulletproofed.

I keep my shoulder pressed against a column and use it to keep cover as I scan the grounds. A flash of movement at the front catches my eye. Two men dressed in black, carrying automatic rifles, make their way toward the front door.

Where the hell is Yakov?

Deep down, I know that if they've broken through our defenses, he won't be alive. I can't understand how anyone found me here. Only a handful of my trusted men know of this location.

One guy is at the front door, and I wait, ready to shoot him the moment he steps through. They can't see where I'm standing. Whoever the fuck these assholes are, they've got real guts to try to kill me in my own fucking home.

The door clicks open, and the first guy steps inside. I shoot him in the head, blood splattering all over the wall behind him. The next guy ducks down out of my view, making it impossible to hit him.

A flash of movement outside draws my attention as a van drives in and pulls up.

Fuck.

At least six men jump out of the back, rushing toward the front door. I focus on the door, ready to hit as many of these bastards as possible. Vera is in danger. I have to protect her no matter the cost.

The first guy comes through the door, and I wait, needing more of them to come into view. Three appear by the door. I strike then, shooting all three of them.

I shoot one in the neck, another in the head, and the last in the chest, but it doesn't kill him. He's wearing a bulletproof vest.

"Where the fuck is he?" another man asks, staying out of view.

I almost jump out of my skin as two hands settle on my arms. "One guy is right there," she whispers into my ear, nodding toward the other side of the sofa, where I can see two feet.

Shit.

There's no easy way out of this. I push her behind me, blocking her between myself and the pillar. I set off a shot and catch his foot, making him yelp. He moves the wrong fucking way, and I shoot him, missing his head by a damn millimeter. It is at that point that I know I'm screwed.

All I can think about is Vera. I push her to the floor as the shot rings out. It feels like time slows to a halt as the bullet travels toward me, hitting me in the chest. A shrill scream rings out, and I know it's Vera. Then, a flurry of gunshots fills the air, along with what sounds like Alexi shouting.

I hit the floor, and my eyes clamp shut. Despite wanting to hold on, I can feel myself slipping away. All I can see is Vera's face gazing at me, bathed in a ring of light, like a halo around her head. She's a beautiful angel watching over me, and I did not protect her. All I can hope is that Alexi is here to save her.

12

VERA

I freeze in a state of panic as Andrei hits the floor. His blood paints the tiled floor a deep red. Before I can rush to him, the man who shot him grabs me around the waist and lifts me off the floor.

A flurry of gunshots rings out, and I glance out the window, noticing three men I recognize from Andrei's home. I try to fight against him, kicking and screaming. "Who the fuck are you?" I shout. Desperate to be released so I can get back to Andrei.

He doesn't respond, speaking Russian to one of the other men. They say they've got what they came for, and their boss will be pleased. I wonder whether Igor was behind this. He told me he would come for Andrei within a week if I hadn't completed my task. It has been a week.

It would be the only reason they'd snatch me.

Does that mean Andrei is dead?

Numbness spreads through my flesh like a disease. Andrei can't be dead, and it would kill me if he were. The man holding me rushes out of the cabin and bundles me into the back of a blacked-out SUV.

The vehicle speeds away from the cabin and away from Andrei. I hope his men get to him in time to save his life. The alternative isn't worth thinking about. I sit in the back of the vehicle for what feels like hours.

A few attempts to shout at the men at the front and demand to know where we are going have failed. All I can think about is Andrei.

He could be dead for all I know. The lump in my throat hurts too much, and my chest aches. The SUV stops at an industrial site on the outskirts of the city.

One man opens the door to the car and yanks me out. I grunt and try to writhe against him, but he's too strong. He picks me up and carries me into the warehouse, taking a left and forcing me into a plain, dark office.

He pushes me into a hard, plastic seat before a rotten, wooden desk. "Wait here," the man who dragged me in here barks, marching out of the room and slamming the door shut behind him.

I glance around the room, trying to learn more about who has me. I've got a good idea who is behind my kidnapping, but Andrei has many enemies.

Andrei.

My stomach twists with nausea as I remember him lying in a pool of blood. They'd shot him in the shoulder and chest. In a short space of time, he means something to me. The first man I ever slept with or even got close enough to care about.

Is Andrei dead?

The sound of the door opening draws my attention. As expected, my uncle, Igor, is standing in the doorway. The look in his eyes sends a shiver down my spine. He's angry that I haven't killed Andrei.

"Hello, Vera," he says, walking to sit behind his desk. He steeples his fingers on top of it and glares at me. "I wish I could congratulate you on your success, but it seems you forgot why Andrei bought you."

"I did not forget."

"Then why did my men see you snuggling close to him when they arrived this morning?"

"It's called acting," I say, tightening my jaw. If my uncle learns I betrayed him, he will kill me. "I had to make him pay for their death. Killing him isn't enough."

He tuts and taps his fingers against the desk. "I told you to take his life swiftly."

I let my eyes sink to the desk and try to play my part. "I know, uncle. It's hard to accept that a swift killing is enough suffering for the suffering he has inflicted on me."

He nods his head. "I understand. It seems he has grown an attachment to you, and this could play to our advantage. My man was as unsuccessful as you were, and I have punished him for that."

I don't glance up, keeping still and unmoving. Andrei is alive. The relief I feel is monumental. A fluttering in my tummy ignites, and warmth thaws the numbness that had inflicted me. "What is it you need me to do?"

He clears his throat. "I assume you had a plan when you were seducing him?"

I nod my head, meeting his gaze. "Yes, sir. I intended to make him believe I cared for him before hurting him. The blow would be far more painful that way."

My uncle smiles. "I taught you well, too well."

I return the smile despite the sickness twisting my gut. Return me to Andrei, and I will make the man who killed my parents pay. It's clear that all this time, I've been blind to the truth. Andrei didn't kill my parents. Igor did.

He kept hitting them when I was out, as I'd be the easiest to manipulate — the youngest girl—the emotional one—who would do anything to avenge her family. My brother and sister would never have fallen for it.

How was I so blind?

Now that I consider it, it makes perfect sense. Igor

is the only person who benefitted once my family died. He took over as *pakhan* to the Saint Petersburg Brotherhood. All the power and money went to him.

Why would Andrei want to kill my family?

He wouldn't have gained anything. All this time, I've believed every word my uncle said, but not anymore. I won't let him use me. I won't rest until he has suffered.

"How is everything back home?" I ask, keeping my tone light. "Are my cousins, Anna and Tiana, well?" I ask, referring to his daughters.

His eyes flash at the mention of his daughters. "Everything is fine at home," he snaps. "Your cousins look forward to reuniting with you once you complete your task." His left eye twitches, and I know he is not telling the truth about my cousins. It wouldn't surprise me if someone has harmed them or they are dead.

He never cared for them as a father should, unlike my father. My dad was more paternal toward Igor's daughters than he ever was. "We intend to get you back into the Petrov household tomorrow morning." He stands for his chair. "When you return, you will tell them you escaped from captured and made it back to the city."

I nod my head. "Yes, uncle."

He sets a device in my hand. "We will listen to every single word, Vera, so do not fuck this up."

"I won't let you down, uncle."

It's important to make sure he doesn't know that my allegiance has changed. If he catches on, I'll be dead, and so will Andrei.

"I need to equip you with some better weapons. Follow me." He walks out of the room, and I trail behind him.

If it weren't for the fact I'm outnumbered here, I would strangle the life out of him right now. Naive is the only way to describe what I was when he convinced me that Andrei Petrov killed them.

A man who may have a ruthless persona and won't shy away from doing what's necessary, but deep down, has a heart of gold. A part of him he showed to me despite my attempts on his life.

I'm desperate to get back to him and ensure he's okay. He may not be dead, but he was shot twice. I was certain he was dead when I saw the bullet hit him in the chest before Igor's men dragged me away from him. If it hadn't been for Andrei's men arriving when they did, he would be dead.

Igor's men have deposited me near Andrei's home. I recognize nothing, but they are sure Andrei and his men will find me.

They have left me in a small but pleasant park. Instead of moving around, I sit in the center of the park. A few kids play on the swings nearby.

My uncle was certain they'd find me since they had been searching for me today. I feel like I'm on a knife-edge, unsure what to do. If I make a mistake, I'll end up being the one who gets cut. I've got to play this right.

Andrei is the one telling the truth in this situation. He's kind and caring, nothing like the man my uncle described him to be. It was all a ruse to make me believe he was the killer.

Igor knew that if I found out he killed them, I wouldn't rest until I'd killed him.

A pair of hands land on my shoulders, and I'm hoisted to my feet. I struggle out of the man's grip, turning to glare at him. His peppered gray hair is dark and messy, and he has tattoos on his neck and arms. I recognize him from Andrei's place.

"Vera, come with me, please," he says, eyes narrowing.

"Who are you?" I ask.

He steps forward. "Demetri, one of Andrei's men."

I observe him for a moment, unsure whether to trust him or not. "Are you going to take me back to him?"

He nods his head. "Yes, he has asked us to find you." He closes his hand around my arm, pulling me toward him. "It is best that you don't deny Andrei Petrov. He can be ruthless to anyone who denies him."

I play along, letting him drag me out of the park. "Okay, I can walk, you know." I hold my hand in the air. He need not drag me back to Andrei as I would willingly sprint to him.

Demetri lets go of me but stays close. "There is no use running, as I'll only catch you."

I nod and walk in front of him, accepting that he will encroach on my personal space until we're behind locked doors. What he doesn't know is I'd never run.

The moment I had sex with Andrei, I knew this wasn't pure lust. Our connection is deep, even if it makes no fucking sense. I was supposed to kill him. That is what I had intended to do when he bought me at that auction and took me home.

It makes me sick to the stomach as I remember the way I watched him sleep, holding that razor over his throat.

What has my uncle turned me into?

Before my family died, I wouldn't even consider hurting a fly, let alone a person. He wielded my grief as a weapon and warped me into someone I no longer recognize.

The man I was supposed to kill has stolen my heart. A heart I believed was too broken to function again, but I feel human for the first time since I lost my family. My uncle thought he had the perfect plan. What he didn't bargain for was that he'd thrust me into the arms of my soul mate.

The numbness eases as Andrei's warmth and kindness thaw my ice-cold exterior. With Andrei, it feels like I might have a future—a chance. A chance I never expected to have again.

13

ANDREI

The ringing in my ears subsides as my eyes flick open. For a moment, I'm stunned and unsure where I am. The pain registers, and the wetness beneath me makes my heart rate speed up.

I bring my hand up to my face, finding it coated in blood—my blood. I shouldn't be alive, but then I see Alexi kneeling by my side. He's got Lyov with him, standing a little way away. And Roman, our brotherhood doctor, kneeling next to him.

"Andrei, can you hear us?" he says, putting pressure on the second wound I took to my chest.

I nod my head, trying to sit up.

He pins me down to the floor. "Don't move. You've lost a lot of blood."

Panic hits me. "Vera, where is she?"

Alexi and Roman exchange glances. "They've taken her."

A flood of adrenaline takes the pain away, and I sit bolt-upright, attempting to get to my feet. I have to find her. Vera is *everything* to me. I can't let them take her.

As I get to my feet, my head swims. Alexi grabs my arm, steadying me. "Chill out, *brat*. Where do you think you are going?"

I shake my head. "I need to find her."

Alexi glances at Lyov. "First, we need to get you back to base and treated. Lyov has information he can give to you once we're there."

I clench my jaw, wishing I could fight against my *sovietnik*, but at the moment, I haven't got the energy. My men are right. The blood loss has drained me, and trying to go after Vera now would be a suicide mission.

If I were to find them, I'd pass out. I glance back at where I'd been lying, grimacing at the puddle of blood. "What brought you guys out here?"

Lyov steps closer. "I found out some troubling information, and we were on our way to tell you when Alexi got a call from Yakov saying you were being ambushed." He pauses a moment.

"Where is Yakov?" I scan the area.

He swallows hard. "Dead."

I'm numb hearing my trusted driver and close friend is dead. He held a low rank in our brotherhood, but he was one man I trusted above all. He was a man

I'd kept close to my side for eight years since I took control. He was the driver for my father, too, when I was a kid. His loss will hurt for a while. There is no time to mourn in the Bratva, even in front of my brothers. It would be seen as a weakness. I nod instead, swallowing the lump in my throat. "Let's get going, then."

Alexi and Roman help me out of the cabin, getting me inside a car. I rest my head back against the headrest, shutting my eyes. The moment they shut, I see her. Vera Popov. The woman who tried to kill me, the woman I crave, and the woman who I'll walk through fire to get back—no matter the consequences.

ROMAN GIVES me my fluids and IV treatment, pulling the needle out. I wince as the site stings, but nowhere near as much as my shoulder hurts. He has patched that up and the wound to my chest without painkillers. I need to be alert if I'm going to get Vera back, and pain meds won't help.

Lyov has been lingering by the doorway, eager to speak with me. I can see it on his face. He steps closer to the bed as Roman walks away. "We've found out who attempted to kill you."

I shift in the bed, wincing at the pain radiating through my shoulder. It may be a flesh wound, but it hurts like a bitch — not as much as it hurts being parted from Vera.

"Who the fuck are they?" I sit up straighter in my chair.

His brow furrows, stepping closer. "The woman you had purchased from the virgin auction is called Vera Popov… As in, Ivan Popov's daughter."

I nod my head. "Yes, I know, she told me."

His mouth falls open for a second before he clears his throat. "Igor Popov is the man behind your attempted murder. He says he has evidence you murdered his brother. He's her uncle."

"I know. Vera's uncle told her I killed her family, which is impossible since I was here in America when it happened." I run a hand across my beard. "They sent Vera to kill me, but she believed me when I told her the truth. She never told me her uncle put her up to it."

He shakes his head. "What don't you know?"

"Where she is," I say

His eyes narrow. "Why does it matter where Vera is?"

I bite the inside of my cheek, wishing I hadn't spoken. Lyov is my spy. We've known each other for years, but I'm uncertain I can trust him with the truth. "No one takes from me," I say, keeping my eyes cold. He can't know how much she means to me—no one can.

"We have the proof Igor Popov killed his brother."

He dips his hand into a briefcase, pulling out some photos.

They show a man standing over the bodies of four people. The guy is covered in blood. I wonder if these were the photos they manipulated to show Vera. "He is trying to expand his power into America." He places the pictures in my hand. "We believe he has had you and your father in his sights ever since he killed Ivan and his family."

"Why us?" I ask.

He shrugs. "The New York Brotherhood is the largest outfit in North America. We're the richest, and greed drives Igor."

"The best plan of action?" I ask.

He sets his hand on the gun on his belt. "Find him and kill him."

I nod. "Sounds good." I stand from the edge of the bed and walk toward my wardrobe, grabbing a shirt.

I wince as I shrug it on before turning and walking toward the bedroom door. Lyov steps into my patch, placing his hand on my good shoulder. "Where the fuck are you going, sir?"

"I will find and kill that bastard," I growl.

He flinches but keeps his hand on my shoulder. "You've been shot twice, less than two hours ago. Let us handle it."

I narrow my eyes at him. "Get the fuck out of my way." If this were any normal situation not involving

Vera, I wouldn't insist on going in my condition. I need to be there when they find her. Otherwise, she might get caught in the crossfire. I won't allow that to happen.

"You aren't in a fit state to accompany us in something so dangerous." He squares his shoulders, trying to assert his dominance. He is walking a fine line with me right now. If he's not careful, I'll batter him for his insolence, even with one arm out of action.

"Out of my way," I command, voice turning dangerous. I bump him with my good shoulder. "Don't get too cocky, Lyov," I warn, marching out of the room.

"I've located her, sir," Alexi says as I walk out of the bedroom straight into the hallway.

"Vera?" I ask.

He nods, and I glance back at Lyov, who is leaning against the door. "Where is she?"

Alexi shrugs and steps to one side, and I feel the blood pumping harder through my veins. Vera is standing in front of me. "Demetri found her, wandering through a nearby park. She said she escaped them and returned to the city."

Vera's eyes meet mine, and I know something is wrong. It's as if she's trying to warn me. Either she has convinced her uncle she's still working for him, or maybe she is still working for him.

However, once she sees the proof that I didn't kill

her family, I'm sure her allegiances will switch for good.

The only thing I can hope is that she trusts me after this. Otherwise, it may end in both our deaths. If she were to stand against me, I'd be in an impossible situation.

As the *pakhan* of the New York brotherhood, I must punish anyone who tries to undermine my power. Death is the only acceptable punishment. I've got a feeling that no matter what, I wouldn't be able to allow her death.

"Thank you, Alexi." I step closer to her, feeling my heart race in my chest. "I'll interrogate her from here." I set my hand on her arm, pulling her close, inhaling her sweet, feminine scent. It's been less than twenty-four hours since I touched her, but damn did I miss her.

"Sir," he says, bowing.

Lyov steps up beside me. "So, you aren't coming to find Igor?"

"No, I need to question Vera."

A knowing smile twists Lyov's lips, but he says nothing. The first time I'd ever seen even a hint of a smile from him. I watch as he walks down the corridor and toward the front door.

"Vera," I breathe her name once we're alone.

"Andrei," she says my name in warning before lifting her top.

A bug is fixed in her bra, under her clothes. I pull

her into my bedroom. "Strip," I command, my voice cold and calculating.

"But, I-I."

"Now," I growl, ensuring my act is convincing. Igor might think he's smart, but he's not.

What did he think I'd purchased a virgin for?

If I act as I'm expected to, sex would be the first thing on my mind. Once I've forced Vera to strip, I'll destroy the bug and give that bastard a message.

Vera licks her bottom lip before unzipping her jeans and pulling them down her hips. Her lacy panties are wet already, and I haven't touched her. "Good, now take off your shirt."

She gives me a questioning look before moving her hand to the buttons on her blouse. I feel the blood rushing south as she reveals her perfect breasts and peaked nipples to me.

I groan, playing up for the man listening to this conversation. As the bug comes into view, I growl. "What the fuck is that?"

I step toward her, and her face pales as I rip the device from her. "Whoever the fuck thought they could snatch my property and then bug her is mistaken. Watch your back." I throw the device on the floor before stamping on it and crushing it to pieces.

Vera gives me a wary look, wondering where we stand.

I step toward her and take her hands in mine.

"Vera," I mutter her name before pulling her close. Her tongue slips into my mouth, and I suck on it, making her moan. The need to claim her tugging at me deep inside, but I know this isn't the time.

"I've got something to show you," I mutter against her lips.

She pulls back and looks into my eyes. "What is it?"

I wince as I pull the photos out of my pocket. "I'm unsure whether you want to see these again without the photo manipulation." Her family's death was brutal, and I don't want to hurt her by bringing the past up.

"The original photos?" she asks, eyes glossy.

I nod, clutching them to my chest. "It is up to you whether you look at them. I can tell you who it was."

"It was my uncle, wasn't it?"

Vera's last surviving relative is Igor Popov, and even his daughters were killed a year ago in a bomb blast aimed at him. I swallow hard. "Yes."

She nods her head and holds out her hands for the photos.

I pass them into her hands and wait, my heart beating out of my chest.

Is she going to trust me now?

Vera returns her gaze to me, and her eyes are burning with fire. "I will kill that bastard." She clenches her hands by her side.

I can't help the warm pride spreading through my

chest as I pull her close, kissing her forehead. "I'll help you."

She pulls back, staring at me like I'm mad. "Why?"

My brow furrows, and I gaze at her momentarily, contemplating the question. "For one, he tried to kill me... As *pakhan*, I can't let that go unanswered." I slip my hands to her waist and squeeze. "For two, I'd do anything for you," I breathe into her ear, making her shiver.

She licks her bottom lip and averts my gaze. I can't believe I uttered those words, but they're true. Thank God no one else is around to hear them. I would lose my reputation as a ruthless and heartless son of a bitch if anyone knew the truth. I care for the woman I purchased.

14

VERA

*M*y uncle will burn in hell for what he did to his own family. Igor killed them. I've been a foolish and blind soldier, working for him, not knowing the truth.

Igor won't lie low for long. Not now he knows I'm compromised.

Andrei has set up a rather public appearance for a charity event this evening. It doesn't sit well with me, as he will draw bloodshed to such a public event.

Andrei assured me that if any of the attendees get shot, they will deserve it. The people attending this so-called charity gala are criminals. The money only goes to a charity in an attempt to launder it.

Most of the so-called charities aren't even real, anyway. The Bratva way of life is despicable and disgusting. I hated it when my father was *pakhan*, and I hate it now.

What surprises me is the way Andrei talks. He seems like he hates it just as much as I do.

"*Krasivaya*, are you ready?" Andrei asks, standing behind me.

I turn to face him, smiling. "How did you get in here?" I glance at the door. I'm sure he couldn't sneak past me.

He turns around and flicks a switch on the wall, opening a door. "Our rooms are adjoining."

I raise an eyebrow. "Why didn't you tell me before?" He smirks and walks toward me. "I wanted to surprise you." He slides his hands onto my waist, and the moment he touches me, I'm a puddle of hot, molten lava.

"Must you touch me right now?" I ask, exasperated by the way one touch sets my skin ablaze.

He tightens his grip on my waist and kisses my neck. "I can't help it. You look stunning in this dress."

My cheeks warm at the compliment. I chose this dress, hoping it would excite Andrei. The plunging neckline offers a teasing view of my cleavage, and the length shows off just enough of my legs without it being too exposing.

"I wish I could rip it off you," he groans, spinning me around and pressing the throbbing length of him into my ass.

I moan, arching my back. "How long until we need to leave?"

He teases his lips against my ear. "We've got five minutes."

"It is long enough," I say, hitching the skirt of my dress up.

He chuckles a low, deep rumble and pushes me forward over the dressing table. "Hold on."

I hold my breath, waiting for him to make a move. He rips my panties off of me, tearing them apart. "No panties for you tonight," he murmurs.

The zip of his pants comes down, and I quiver in anticipation, my juice dripping down my thighs.

"I want you to come on my cock, *Printsessa*." He thrusts the entire length inside me with one push, making me scream.

His hand connects with my ass, spanking each check with an erotic slap that sends so much pleasure through me that it feels like I might combust already. There's no doubt in my mind he will make me come with not much effort.

It's building as his hand slips down between my thighs, and he rubs my clit in circles, quickening me toward the edge. The hard length of his cock pounding into me is heaven. If I could die now, I'd die happy.

Sex with this man is beyond anything I ever could have imagined. I'd watched porn before, but nothing ever came across as this intense, this needy. It's as if he is a wild animal trying to breed me. The grunts and groans he makes are in line with that—animalistic and ferocious.

I've thought about the consequences and what it means to be fucking like this without protection. It is wild. Andrei should take precautions, but perhaps the bastards who trained me slipped me contraception without me knowing.

I moan as he slaps my ass again, no doubt painting it red. The sting intensifies my pleasure, and I know I will come any second. "Fuck, Andrei…"

"That's it, come all over my cock," he growls, and it's all it takes to send me tumbling into pure bliss.

I'm slammed with the force of an intense orgasm, heating me and blinding me all at once. The breath from my lungs escapes me as I pant, trying to gain a grip on reality.

Andrei grunts behind me, thrusting one last time inside of me and holding himself so deep. I can feel his cock twitching inside of me, spilling his seed as deep as possible. My thighs quiver as I realize his cum will drip out of me all night.

"Hold tight," he says.

My brow furrows as he shoves his hand into his pocket and pulls out a sex toy. It looks like an odd-shaped dildo. "What are you going to do with that?"

His smirk is almost wicked as he pulls his cock out of me and shoves it in place. "I want you to wear it tonight," he says, spanking my ass again.

I moan, turned on again, despite reaching climax a few moments ago.

He grabs something else out of his pocket, and I gasp. The toy vibrates deep inside of me, making me quiver.

"I will control you all night, Vera." His eyes are wild and dark.

I shake my head, trying to ignore the sensations as he turns up the vibration level. "Aren't we supposed to be focusing on catching my uncle?"

He shrugs. "Yes, but my men will be there for that."

I gasp as he presses another button, turning the vibration even higher. "I can't wear this tonight. I'll orgasm at the table."

He smiles wider, kissing my lips. "That is the point, Vera." His hand entangles with mine as he switches the vibrator off, stowing the controller in his pocket. "Come on."

"Wait." I jerk him to a stop. "I need to put new panties on."

He pulls on my hand, forcing me to walk with him. "No panties."

Fuck.

I can't sit at a table with strangers with no panties on, his cum dripping out of me, and a fucking vibrator shoved in my pussy. I groan to myself as he holds me closer, walking me out of his house.

Andrei loves to be in control, and there's no use

fighting him on this. Not to mention, deep down, it may be a little exciting doing something like that in public.

Once we're in the car, he turns to me. "Do you remember your virgin training?"

"Yes, why?"

He nods. "Act as you were trained to, as I can't have people talking about the way I treat you."

"That makes sense," I say, gazing out of the window.

I don't speak the question on my mind, knowing it may be a step too far. If I am Andrei's slave, does that mean that is all I can ever be to him?

Andrei is the *pakhan* to the powerful Bratva brotherhood. If he were to break the rules on slavery, they would see it as a weakness. Perhaps, if I were to get pregnant, it would change things. Bratva is big on family, and a *pakhan* being provided an heir gives stability to its leadership.

"What are you thinking?"

I turn to Andrei, and he's staring at me with an adoring gaze. It makes my chest ache. The last man I saw looked at me like that was my father.

It was different circumstances, but my father was a very loving man behind closed doors, much like Andrei. "Nothing much."

He doesn't look convinced by my answer, and I bite my lip. He pulls the remote control out of his pocket. "Tell me, Vera."

My cheeks heat as I shake my head. It's too embarrassing to tell him what I was thinking. I was thinking of a future with him. He may not feel the way I feel.

He turns it on, and I gasp, arching my back as the vibrations hit the perfect spot deep inside of me. "Fuck."

He chuckles, shifting closer to me in the back of the vehicle. "I can't fuck you in here."

"Why are you doing this?"

He cups my chin in his hand and brushes his lips against mine. "I want to know everything about you."

His words send a shiver down my spine, and warmth pools in my stomach.

He kisses me. "Tell me what you were thinking about."

The warmth in my cheeks increases. "I was just wondering whether I always have to act like a slave around you in public."

He drops my chin and moves away from me as if I've said something I shouldn't have. The remote switches off, and he leaves me feeling empty and ashamed. Am I getting too bold to think this could ever be something more? I am a slave, and he is my master.

He wants to dominate my body, and that is all. It's my fault I haven't guarded my heart against the charming *pakhan*. Sometimes, the things he says hit right to my core. He told me he'd do anything for me.

Is that something a man says to a sexual partner? I wouldn't know, considering he is my first.

Every moment spent with him, the more I can't imagine living my life without him in it. If that means I have to be his sex slave for the rest of my life, so be it.

We're two emotionally broken people with so much baggage. We can't dare to hope we'd fix each other.

The car comes to a stop outside of an old building. A steady stream of well-dressed and elegant people meander inside, handing over invitations to the muscle-bound bouncers dressed in black.

Andrei takes my hand. "Remember, play your part, Vera."

"Of course," I reply, forcing a weak smile.

His dark eyes flash with approval as he gets out of the car first.

I wait for him to come around to my side and open the door.

"Out," he barks in a detached tone.

I was expecting to hear the change in his voice, but somehow it hurts. I've let myself get carried away over this man— a man who owns me.

I'd heard women get attached to the men who take their virginity, but this is deep and clawing. If he doesn't feel it, too, it will hurt like hell, but I'm used to pain and sadness at this point.

Rejection is the least of my worries. First, I need

to focus on killing my uncle. I haven't spoken about it to Andrei, but I want to be the one to end his life. The need to avenge my parents, brother, and sister is still very much alive inside of me.

Andrei passes the bouncer his entry ticket, and the bouncer gives me an odd look, which entices a deep growl from Andrei. The bouncer, who has to be six-feet-eight tall, pales, nodding for us to go inside.

Let the games begin.

15

ANDREI

a buzz of chatter surrounds the hall as Vera sits by my side, placing her hands in her lap. She's doing well at keeping up appearances, slipping into her role as an obedient slave effortlessly.

A few attendees tonight gave me funny looks when I sat her down by my side at the main table.

It's seen as bad taste to allow a slave to dine with you, but I would not let her leave my side this evening. There's too much danger to both of us to be apart. She's more beautiful than any of the other women here anyway, slave or not.

Vera is tense. I can sense she wants to be on guard and alert, but she's bound by duty to keep her head bowed and eyes downcast.

This charity event is boring as fuck, and they have sat me with a load of crooked politicians on either side of me and opposite me. I slip my hand into my pocket and tap one button on the remote.

Vera jumps in her seat, eyes coming up for a half-second before she remembers where she is.

I didn't reply to her question in the car, although it wasn't a question. I forced her to tell me what she was thinking. It caught me off guard. My heart beats faster as I remember the hurt in her eyes when I didn't reply.

The last thing I want to do is treat her like a slave, but caring about a woman when you're *pakhan* of a Bratva brotherhood is dangerous.

My enemies have been trying to kill me for years. Fear of being killed no longer registers in my mind. I have to prepare for every minute of every day, but Vera dying is a different story.

I couldn't imagine losing her. She's the most precious thing to come into my life since I can remember. We've both been through a lot. I watch her as she ignores the sensations my vibrator is pulsing through her. She has such control over herself. It's admirable.

We are similar in so many ways. Our self-control, unless it comes to each other. We're both ruthless and strong when it comes to what we want.

She would have killed me that day in the bedroom while I slept. It was only her moment of hesitation that saved me.

I flick the setting higher, and she squeezes her

thighs together. Her cheeks are bright pink. I love seeing her that color and knowing I'm the reason—well, the toy I control inside her.

I groan under my breath as my cock thickens in my tight boxer briefs, leaking into the fabric. She's too beautiful, and I'm too greedy whenever she's near.

I love being able to make her feel good with this toy without even touching her.

She bites her bottom lip in a way that makes me want to growl, lift her onto the table, and give everyone a fucking good show. At least it would liven up this God-awful party.

I switch the settings up again, and she's getting close to orgasm. Her chest heaves with every breath she takes, and her fingers claw into her thighs. I notice her eyes flutter shut for a moment and her lips part.

She's trying to control her reactions, but it's no longer working. In a moment, I will have to insist we both go to the bathroom. I'm aching to be inside of her.

Until a voice sounds in my earpiece, breaking my concentration and lust-filled state. "We've spotted the target, and he appears to be in attendance tonight with a date," Alexi says.

I clench my jaw, knowing he's attempting to keep the heat off him. His men will be the ones to take me out for him. Vera will be targeted, too, considering everything he's done to her family thus far.

Vera was right. A charity event isn't the place or

time to be experimenting with a sex toy, but I couldn't help myself. I switch it off and grab her hand. "Look at me."

She does as I say. Her eyes dilate with such longing and pleasure that I almost forget what I was about to say.

"He's here," I mutter under my breath, glancing at the other people sat at our table. None of them are paying much attention to us.

The haze in her irises clears, flooding with rage. I see the way her jaw clenches along with her fists.

"Stay calm." I set my hand on the back of her neck in a possessive move and squeeze, making sure we keep up appearances.

I set my lips on hers and murmur against them. "We don't know Igor's plan yet, so make sure you keep in character."

She lets her eyes drop to her lap. I clear my throat and focus on the food, which must have arrived while playing with the toy stuffed deep inside my Vera.

"Eat," I command, picking up my cutlery. Vera does the same, shoveling tiny pieces of food into her mouth.

I scan the room with careful attention as I eat. Even though I've never met Igor in person, the photos should be enough to recognize him.

A tall figure entering the main hall with a young blonde woman on his arm catches my eye. It's him.

There's no doubt about it. Our eyes meet momentarily, and he dares to smirk at me.

Motherfucker.

He tried to kill me, and now he's smirking at me. The alpha inside me wants to rise and fight him here and now. Do away with this sneaky bullshit and pummel him to a pulp for everything he has done for everyone to see.

I could do it, but my actions would cause a raucous. Everyone here knows who I am and what I'm capable of, but seeing it is another story. This man was behind my father's death. My intuition is telling me he is the reason for my suffering and Vera's.

The last thing I want to do is fuck this all up. The intention is to find out if Igor was the one who targeted my dad. Then, I will murder him without hundreds of witnesses. We have him right where we want him.

The asshole finds his seat, holding the chair out for the woman accompanying him. She can't be much older than eighteen, and she looks terrified.

Vera has slipped back into the submissive slave, but she's not eating anymore.

I press my finger to my ear and murmur. "Any news?"

"We think he's gearing up for a bang, but no movement yet."

Although I didn't know he'd have the guts to show

his face at the event, it's what we expected. "Stay put. I'm going to the bathroom," I say to Vera.

She says nothing. Instead, she keeps eating.

I'm uneasy leaving her out in the open, but it's the best way to lure him out. Not to mention, my men are on guard stationed in the gallery above the main dining hall.

If Igor believes she is still working for him, he might approach her. In any other case, he may try to hurt her, but my men won't let that happen.

I head as if I'm going to the bathroom, stopping when I'm out of sight and turning to glance back into the main dining hall. Igor sits with his guest, but his eyes are fixed on Vera.

I watch him stand from his chair and walk toward her. His steps are slow and deliberate. The man is a slithering snake. A weasel that doesn't deserve to breathe the same air as my Vera.

I watch him speak, and she glances up at him. From here, it's unclear whether he's angry with her or assumes she's getting the job done.

Igor won't take my message to him lightly.

I see him grab hold of her shoulder, and it's not a friendly move. A woman sitting close by says something to him.

Vera looks uncomfortable and unsure, glancing between the woman at the table and her uncle.

Fuck this.

I walk back toward the table at speed, marching

toward the asshole who tried to kill me. "Igor," I say, keeping my voice deep and cold.

He spins toward me and flashes me a fake smile. "Andrei, I was just speaking with your slave." He nods his head toward Vera.

"Did I give you permission to speak with my property?" I ask, making sure my tone is anything but polite. The guy is fucking with me, and I can't let it slide, not here.

He holds his hands up. "I'm sorry, but I wanted to speak to my niece."

A few whispers and gasps break out around us. Slaves shouldn't be related to Bratva members. Even though Igor is the *pakhan* of a Russian brotherhood, he's well known here in America.

Most would see it as disrespectful for another *pakhan* to own a woman whose family is Bratva. He's playing a game with me, trying to get me to release her. "I was not aware she was your family when I purchased her," I say, keeping my voice even.

He crosses his arms over his chest and squares up to me. "I don't doubt that is true, but I would like to discuss the matter." He holds out a hand, signaling toward his table. "Would you join me for a moment?"

I grit my teeth together. This could be a trap, and it smells of one, too.

Igor enjoys every second of this, as his dark green eyes hold too much amusement.

I give him a nod.

"Follow me."

Vera goes to stand, but he sets his hand on her shoulder harder than I'd like. She falls back into her seat. "Stay here, Vera, and let the men speak."

I give her a short nod, and she glances down at her lap. As I walk away with Igor, I keep glancing back, noticing the woman next to her is trying to talk to her. Now she knows Vera's not truly a low-life slave, she has started to pay attention to her.

"What do you want, Igor," I snap before making it to the table.

He turns and smirks at me. "I think you know what I want."

I do, and it will not happen. Igor won't get the better of me here on my turf. "You can't kill me in front of all these people."

His smirk only widens. "Watch me."

I realize all of a sudden that he wanted me to stand, making me an easy target. It takes a split-second reaction as I dive beneath a table, shocking the other guests.

A gunshot sounds, and it ricochets off the ground, inches from where I was standing.

Vera.

I crawl on my hands and knees beneath the table as screams break out around me. A gunshot claps out, followed by another, no doubt trying to clear the hall so they can find me. All I can think about is Vera, who is a sitting duck.

I can't lose her. I won't lose her. She's not my slave but the love of my life, and I will protect her with everything I've got.

The truth I've been ignoring hits me like a freight train—I love her.

16

VERA

*T*he woman sitting next to me suddenly collapses into her food, blood spurting from her head in a horrifying spray. The screams and shouts of panic echo throughout the room, blending into a chaotic symphony as people scramble from their seats and flee for their lives.

My heart pounds in my chest, threatening to burst as I frantically scan the room in search of Andrei. Just moments ago, he was standing to my right, and now he's vanished into thin air. Fear grips me as the thought of him being shot takes hold. I can't bear the idea of losing him.

Where is he?

As if on cue, another gunshot pierces the air, missing me by a mere inch and shattering a nearby vase into jagged shards. In that split second, I know I have to find cover if I want to survive. With adrenaline coursing through my veins, I dive under the nearest table, hoping it will provide some semblance of protection. Bullets whiz past me, their deadly intentions thwarted by the chaos of the moment.

Crawling on my hands and knees beneath the long table, I navigate the dimly lit room, desperately trying to retrace the path where Andrei had stood only moments ago. Uncle Igor has marked me as a target, adding my name to his hit list. But his men, they are terrible shots. It's my only saving grace.

The truth of my identity has been exposed to the world by Uncle Igor himself, and if we manage to escape this deadly encounter, it won't be long before everyone knows. The revelation will force Andrei to make a choice, one dictated by the Bratva code. Will he release me, as the pakhan, or will he keep me trapped in this dangerous web?

The thought of freedom from slavery should bring solace, not despair, but deep down, it's leaving Andrei behind that fills me with dread. If he lets me go, where will I even go? Back to Russia, where I am utterly alone? All I desire is to be with Andrei because I love him with every fiber of my being.

A sudden gunshot shatters the tense silence, causing my heart to lurch into my throat. I freeze, my body going rigid when I hear the unmistakable sound of footsteps approaching my hiding place. Each step reverberates on the cold, tiled floor, growing louder and closer. Whoever it is, they exude an air of confidence and fearlessness, marking them as either Uncle Igor himself or one of his loyal henchmen.

I know I can't stay trapped in this hall any longer. Determination fuels my every move as I continue to crawl, inch by agonizing inch, along the length of the table. My only hope is to reach the end undetected and slip away into the shadows, praying that I can escape this nightmare unscathed.

The room has fallen into an unsettling silence, causing my heart to race and my blood pressure to surge. The deafening sound of my own heartbeat resonates in my ears, a constant reminder of the danger lurking nearby.

Coming to a halt at the end of the table, I cautiously peek beneath the tablecloth, my eyes fixated on the door just a few feet away. It's my best shot at escaping this dire situation. The thought of running fills me with apprehension, knowing that it could lead to dire consequences. But if I stay put, I know they'll discover my hiding place soon enough.

With a sense of urgency, I quietly slip off my heels and leave them concealed under the table. There's no way I can make a successful escape with them hindering my every step. As I do so, my uncle's voice echoes through the room in Russian, commanding his men to find me.

A loud clash interrupts the silence, and I steal a quick glance back to witness the chaos unfolding as tables are overturned, starting from the opposite end.

Fuck.

Panic surges through my veins. Time is running out, and I must make a decision now.

I close my eyes, take a deep breath, and launch myself towards the door in a sprint.

The sound of a man's voice shouting, "There she is!" echoes behind me, fueling my adrenaline-fueled escape.

A bullet grazes the door frame just as I slip out into the dimly lit corridor. The cold, rough tiles beneath my bare feet offer little comfort as I push myself to run for dear life.

The menacing thump of heavy shoes closing in on me echoes through the corridor, urging me to push harder and faster. If Igor catches up to me, it will all be over. Thoughts of Andrei flood my mind. We both need to get out of here before it's too late. The whereabouts of his men from the brotherhood, stationed nearby to intercept anyone on my uncle's side, remain a mystery.

Taking a right turn, I sprint down the corridor, refusing to look back. This place is unfamiliar to me, and I cannot afford to lose my way amidst the chaos. Every door, every turn, blurs together in my mind, but I press on, determined to outrun my pursuers.

Nothing looks familiar to me from when we arrived, and I come to a fork in the corridor, unsure which way to go. A shout close behind me forces me to turn right.

As I run, it gets darker, and I suspect I've gone deeper into this place. A room at the end of the corridor catches my eye, and I slip inside, hoping to give my chasers the slip.

Taking a moment to catch my breath, I survey my surroundings and realize I've stumbled upon an office. The fading sound of footsteps charging past the room washes over me, offering a brief respite from the relentless pursuit. A sigh of relief escapes my lips, but I know the danger is far from over.

My legs are aching, and my chest is tight from sprinting. There was a time when I was fit, but after a year cooped up in a basement trained to be a dutiful slave, running isn't easy.

I try to get my breathing under control, knowing it is too raspy and loud. Even though I've given Igor's men the slip for the moment, I'm not out of danger yet. My heart is pounding against my rib cage as I open the door and slip back into the corridor.

Finding Andrei is the only thing on my mind at the moment. I've got no idea where I am or how to get back to the exit of this building. As I approach the dining hall once more, the sound of my uncle's voice pierces the air.

"Andrei, did you really think you could hide from me like a coward?"

I freeze as ice-cold dread spreads through my veins. Igor has got Andrei. I poke my head around the door jamb and glance inside to see him pointing his gun at Andrei. Andrei has his gun pointed at Igor in return. To my relief, they are the only ones in here.

"Stop," I shout, stepping forward into the room to divert my uncle's attention.

My uncle doesn't even spare me a glance as he speaks, his eyes locked onto Andrei. "What do you think you're doing, Vera?"

Ignoring his question, I confront him directly. "You tried to kill me."

His gaze remained fixed on Andrei as he responds to me. "What else was I supposed to do to someone who had turned against me?"

Andrei, his eyes wide with panic, pleads with me. "Vera, please, stay back."

I shake my head, ignoring him. "I wouldn't have turned against you if you hadn't murdered my family," I declare, a lump forming in my throat. The intensity of my hatred for the man before me is incomprehensible.

My mind drifted back to that pivotal moment when I had almost slit Andrei's throat. Igor had driven me to the brink, manipulating me. If I had succumbed and killed Andrei, an innocent man, I would have died too, never uncovering the truth about my uncle until it was too late - buried six feet under.

My demise had always been part of his twisted plan. If Andrei's men had carried it out, the whole ordeal would have appeared cleaner. Igor could have claimed his presence in New York was for revenge against his niece, solidifying his position as the pakhan of the New York brotherhood.

"Finally caught on, Vera," he scoffs, shaking his head. "The gullible woman who believes every word her uncle says."

I clench my fists tightly by my sides, feeling foolish for having fallen for his lies. This despicable man doesn't even bother to deny his involvement in the deaths of his own flesh and blood. "I'll kill you," I spit, seething with rage.

He laughs as if that's the stupidest thing he's ever heard. "Vera, you couldn't kill anyone."

Gritting my teeth, I retort, "I'd make an exception for you."

"Vera, get the fuck out of here," Andrei warns. "Leave this to me."

I shake my head defiantly, narrowing my eyes at my uncle. "I need to be the one to do it."

Andrei's eyes widen. "Watch out! Behind you!" he shouts.

Too late. One of my uncle's men has silently approached from behind, seizing me in his grip. I struggle desperately to break free from his clutches.

Then, I feel the chilling touch of a knife's edge against my throat. I swallow hard, a sharp stinging pain as the serrated blade nicks my skin.

Andrei lunges towards me, but the ominous sound of a gun being cocked freezes him in his tracks. "Not another fucking step, Petrov, or she dies," Igor's states.

Blood trickles down my neck and onto my chest, making me shiver. Having seen the images of Igor standing over his own brother's lifeless body, I have no doubts about the validity of his threat.

Andrei's eyes blaze with a mixture of fury and concern, fixated on the cut at my neck. His muscles tense beneath his shirt and jacket, his jaw clenched. Andrei isn't accustomed to blindly following orders, no matter the circumstances.

My uncle has the upper hand, and it's my fault. I could have stayed out of trouble If I hadn't let my emotions rule me. Now, we're at a disadvantage. Andrei tried to warn me, and I ignored him.

"Gun down, Andrei," Igor commands.

Andrei glances between the man holding me and me and back to Igor a few times, indecision burning in his dark brown eyes.

Then, to my shock, I witness an unexpected sight. Andrei relentes. He lowers his gun, carefully placing it on the floor, and raises his hands in surrender.

My uncle has won unless Andrei has something up his sleeve.

17

ANDREI

"Gun down," Igor commands, narrowing his eyes at me in a warning. The other man's grip tightens on Vera as his boss speaks.

My heart pounds so hard it feels like it might burst out of my chest as I stare at Vera in Igor's man's arms with a knife to her throat. One move, and he can cut her open, ending her life before I can so much as make it within ten feet of her.

The blood trickling down her neck makes me mad with rage. Seeing anyone else touch her makes me insane, let alone hurt her.

For the first time since we met, she's scared. I can detect it in her beautiful emerald eyes and the way her nostrils are flaring. It's her expression that makes my decision easy.

I kneel and set my gun on the floor, holding my hands out in universal surrender. "Let Vera go, Igor."

I hold my hands up. "This is between you and me, not her."

"Give her to me," he commands, grabbing Vera from his man and passing the gun into his hand. I wince as he brings the knife back to her throat, digging it in harder. A rivulet of blood trickles down her neck and onto her chest. The uncontrollable beast inside me roars. I never let go of my control, but this man is hurting the woman I love.

"This has everything to do with her," he snarls. "She was supposed to kill you for me. Instead, she's turned into your fucking whore."

I grit my teeth, hating that he disrespects the woman I love. This man is the lowest of the low. He killed his flesh and blood. He won't hesitate to repeat that, and I know the severity of the situation we're in right now.

The only thing up my sleeve is a knife. I've always been good at knife throwing—the best in North America. However, the pressure of the situation is different from anything I've encountered before. The risk of getting it wrong is too high. "What do you want?" I ask, attempting to stall even though I know what he wants.

"I'm here for blood, Andrei."

I narrow my eyes at him. "What have I done to you?"

He loosens his grip on Vera. "Nothing. I want to expand and take control here in America. You hold

the most power here and have done for a long while."
He shrugs. "It's not personal."

"Why would you want to kill your niece?"

He tightens his grip on her again, digging the
serrated blade into her skin. I wince at the sight of
more blood dripping down her pale neck. "She's no
longer needed and didn't even do as she was supposed
to." He shakes his head. "All the years of training and
planning, and she fucked it all up," he spits.

"If you let her go, I'll come willingly."

He barks out a laugh. "Bullshit. If I let Vera go,
you will fight me until I'm dead." He shakes his head.
"I'm not stupid, Andrei. You've got age on your
side."

I realize there is no reasoning with him. "What
are you going to do then?"

He flicks his eyes between Vera and me. "I want
you to come forward and kneel with your hands
behind your back. Then, my man will tie your
hands."

I glare at him for a moment before switching my
attention to Vera. Her eyes are wide and begging. I
know she doesn't want me to do as he says, but I can't
stand by while he kills her. With a nod, I step forward
toward them.

"Turn around," he barks, setting my teeth on
edge. I follow no one's commands, but I've got no
fucking choice right now. It goes against my nature to
turn around.

"Fillip, tie him up with this," he says, chucking him a rope.

A flutter of hope ignites in my chest as I slip the knife down my sleeve closer to my wrist. If I can take out this man and get his gun, we have a chance.

His rough hands grab at my shoulders hard, and with a flick of my wrist, I let the knife drop into my hand. It takes him by surprise as I push the knife deep into his heart, killing him with one blow.

"Fuck," Igor shouts as I grab the gun and aim at his head.

His eyes narrow. "You wouldn't risk hitting Vera, would you?" He gets Vera even further in front of him.

"I've never missed before," I say, staring him out.

He is right. It's too fucking close, and although I'm a great shot, I don't want to risk him moving Vera at the last second.

"She will be dead before the bullet makes it to me," Igor says.

He can slice her open quicker than the bullet will meet its mark. We stand in a deadlock, and hours tick by as I wait. "What now?" I ask, breaking the silence.

"I'm not giving her up," he growls.

"You let her go, and we fight man to man, fist to fist."

He laughs. "Andrei, you can beat me in a fistfight. I'm not stupid."

Cold dread slices through me as I try to move

closer out of sheer desperation. "Not another fucking step."

Vera whimpers as he tightens the knife to her skin, cutting her deeper. I hold my free hand up. "Okay, don't hurt her."

"Why would you do this to me, uncle?" She asks.

He grabs hold of her throat and turns her to face him, keeping the knife pressed to her chest.

"My brother always had the perfect fucking family and was always the perfect fucking son. When he became *pakhan* of the brotherhood after our father died, I hated him." Vera keeps her hands behind her back, twisting something in her palm. "I hated all of you. Ivan and his perfect little family. I knew you were the weakest and would help me end Andrei." He shakes his head. "Looks like I was wrong about that because you can't keep your fucking clothes on."

"My father loved you, and so did my mother." She shakes her head. "You're pathetic."

I watch as Vera's hand swipes across him. She has the razor from the bathroom in her hand. She cuts him across the face, forcing him to let go of her long enough to break away from him.

Igor staggers back in shock. "Bitch," he spits, grabbing the knife he had been holding from the floor and rushing after her.

She dashes away from him as he slashes the large serrated knife through the air. I cock the gun and shoot, aiming at him. To my horror, the gun isn't even fucking loaded.

Vera dashes toward an exit as Igor trails behind her with crazed eyes, wielding his blade.

She's only got a razor, and a nutcase is chasing after her. I follow them in a sprint, desperate to save her from him.

I need to get to her before he catches her. Vera is agile, but Igor is stronger than her. He can overpower her. I rush out of the dining hall to hear a scream that sends my heart into my throat.

Vera.

I could lose everything in a matter of seconds. The fear of losing the woman I love makes me crazy. The moment I rush into the main hall, my body tense. Igor is looming over her with his knife pressed to her throat.

I dash toward him, too far away to stop the inevitable. Igor notices me and smirks. It ignites a fury inside of me so great as I speed up toward him.

While I distract him, Vera kicks him in the gut, forcing him back into the wall. He falls over, and I know we've got him now.

The pride flooding me at her strength hits me in the chest, warming me. I grab hold of Igor's shirt and pull him to his feet. Rage has grabbed hold of me and is in the driving seat now — everything this man has done to me, hitting me all at once.

I slam my fist into his face so hard I hear his nose

crack — a river of blood flooding from it onto his lip. I punch him again, bloodying his face.

With a tremendous amount of force, I smash him into the ground, placing my foot on his throat and choking him. "I have one question before you die," I growl.

"What?" he spits a mouthful of blood out.

"Did you blow my father up?" I ask, holding my breath as I wait for a reply.

He smirks at me, making me sick to my stomach. "Yes, this plan has been in place for three years. We didn't expect a thirty-year-old man to step up to the plate and take charge." He tries to break from my grip, but I hold fast. "We expected you to be dead within a year, but you stepped up and took charge."

I've had enough of this bastard. Igor opens his mouth to speak again. My vision blurs red as I slam my boot into his jaw, cracking it in two. Igor's face goes limp, and his eyes blur with pain.

Blood paints my fists as I grab his collar again and bring my hand back to hit him. The need to make him hurt as much as he hurt us drives me.

My father was all I had in this world, and he took him from me. When I saw him hurt my Vera, it was the last fucking straw.

A small, soft hand closes around mine, and my reaction is to bring my fist back to punch. Vera doesn't flinch, staring at me with a steely gaze. "Let me finish him," she says.

I shake my head, knowing what it would do to her if she took the plunge today and killed a man. It would rip her apart to kill a man, even though she hates him. "You've never killed before, don't start now."

Her jaw clenches, and the fire in her eyes only deepens. "I need this, Andrei."

I swallow hard and glance back at the bloodied excuse of a man in front of me. He killed my father, too. It's only fair that we end him together. "Together?" I ask.

She gives me a weak smile and nods. "Together."

I watch her as she kneels to grab Igor's blade from the floor and hold it up above his heart.

His eyes are wide and fearful, but he can't beg for his life because I've broken his jaw. He tries to move it but can't. I kneel beside her and wrap my hand around hers. "On three. One, two, three." We both thrust together, driving the knife deep into our tormentor's heart.

Blood bubbles up into his mouth, spilling down the side of his chin as he falls into a crumpled heap on the floor.

A gunshot rings out, and in a split second, I see it traveling toward Vera. I block her with my body, wrapping my arms around her as the bullet hits me square in the back.

We fall to the floor, coated in Igor's and my blood.

Vera cries my name, "Andrei." She remains above me, gripping my face in her hands. "Stay with me."

I can't register what she's saying. All I know is that she is stunning. Another shot has me tensing, bringing me back to the present.

To my relief, Lyov has shot the man who shot me. I relax as Roman comes rushing into the room behind him. It's about time some of my men helped us out. Alexi comes dashing down behind him with a gun in his hand, too. They're all bloodied and bruised, no doubt ambushed by Igor's men.

Vera is safe, and that's all that matters. I return my gaze to her tear-stained face. "Don't cry. Everything is okay."

She swallows hard. "You're not okay."

"Don't worry, Printsessa. I will be fine."

She shakes her head. "You've been shot," she says, holding her hand over the wound tightly.

"Roman will get me up and running in no time."

Alexi approaches us and kneels beside me, smiling at Vera. "He will be fine. Roman is the best doctor I know."

"He's the only doctor you know, Alexi," Lyov says

"Touché."

Lyov approaches. "Let's try to get him to his feet."

Alexi gets one side and Lyov on the other, helping me up. My head swims, but I can walk. Vera slides to my side, wrapping an arm around me and trying to help.

"Thanks, Lyov. If it weren't for you, we'd both be dead."

He gives me a nod. "It was nothing, sir."

"Vera, this is Lyov, one of my spies," I say, introducing them.

"Nice to meet you," she says.

He grunts and nods, eyes narrow.

"Vera is the daughter of Ivan Popov, and I'm not comfortable keeping her as a slave anymore. She will be a guest of mine for now," I announce.

Vera glances up at me with wide eyes. "Why would you release me when you paid so much?"

Alexi steps forward, placing a hand on my back. "Because he has a heart of gold that he doesn't want anyone to know about, that's why."

I glance at Lyov, who is lingering. "Don't worry, boss. I've known it for years," he says.

Roman approaches. "Sir, we need to get you back and into the operating theater as soon as possible."

Vera reluctantly lets go of me as Lyov gets on one side and Alexi on my other. "Roman, walk with Vera," I instruct.

"Sir," he bows his head, and we make our way out of the building.

The police will be here, but they won't stop us. The detectives eye us as we climb onto the pavement and walk toward the SUV. It will be put down to a random shooting, and nothing of the truth will be revealed in the press.

They will register the infiltrators as Igor and his men, which is the truth for once. I wince as my men help me into the back of the SUV. Vera slides in on the other side and sits closer, pressing a hand against my forehead. "You're burning up," she murmurs.

"It may have something to do with your hands on me," I mutter.

She shakes her head, a whisper of a smile playing at her lips. She doesn't smile often, but it lights up my day and thaws out my heart when she does.

I hope to make her smile every single day from now on. I slip my right hand behind her neck and pull her lips to mine, kissing her. "My Vera," I breathe against her lips.

She moans against my mouth, "Yours."

Hearing her tell me she's mine reaffirms everything. We're made for each other—two broken people finding each other in the weirdest ways. It's laughable how fate has a way of screwing with you.

18

VERA

*T*ears prickle my eyes as I watch Andrei disappear into the operating theater. Blood stains his clothes and the bedding.

They shot him close to his heart, and the bullet is still inside of him. Roman, the brotherhood doctor, needs surgery to get it out.

I want him taken to a hospital and treated, but that's against the Bratva code.

If he went to the hospital, they would ask questions about how he got shot. There's a high chance of it all going wrong. I can't lose him.

I sink into one of the chairs outside and let my head fall backward. Stress, panic, and pure fear are ruling me at the moment.

Roman even said it might take up to two hours to perform the surgery. Those two hours will be the longest of my life.

"Vera, how are you holding up?" Alexi asks, trailed by Lyov.

I smile at Alexi, a friendly guy and good friends with Andrei. Lyov is cold and harsh—I've never seen him smile, not once.

I return my attention to the door Andrei has disappeared behind. "Not great."

Alexi takes a seat next to me and sets a hand on my shoulder. "He will be okay."

"How do you know?" I ask, staring into his unique hazel eyes.

He shrugs. "Andrei always pulls through."

It doesn't instill me with much reassurance. There will always be that one time when Andrei won't pull through.

Lyov takes the other seat and crosses his arms over his chest. "Andrei cares about you."

The statement hangs in the air, and I shift.

Alexi chuckles. "He cares about her? Haven't you seen the way he looks at her ever since that auction? He fucking adores her."

My cheeks heat hearing Andrei say that.

Lyov grunts, and his face is unreadable.

Alexi gets up and claps him on the shoulder. "Duty calls, but can you keep Vera company for me?" He winks at me.

Lyov looks less than amused but nods in reply. An awkward silence settles between us for a few minutes until he breaks it. "Vera, I hope you will watch over him."

The sentiment coming from him startles me a little. "Of course."

He looks a little less troubled. "Andrei is a difficult man to get through to, but I hope he will live a little now he's met you." There's a whisper of a smile tugging at his lips. "The guy has never given two shits about anyone as much as he does about you."

I slide my bottom lip between my teeth, wondering what to say. "Do you think Andrei will be okay?"

Lyov chuckles a deep rumble beside me. "Andrei's been through worse than a bullet wound before and come out the other end."

"He has been in the operating theater a while."

Lyov sets a hand on top of mine and squeezes. "He's been in there for under half an hour, and Roman said he might be in surgery for two hours." He shakes his head. "How about we grab some pizza? Then, once we're back, he will be out?"

I glance between Lyov and the door. It would help the time pass quicker, but the thought of leaving the building makes me sick to my stomach. "I can't."

He nods and stands. "Okay, I'll get someone to grab the pizza and bring it here."

I can't help but smile at how the cold, brooding spy is opening up. He's always seemed so quiet. For the first time, I see him soften and become more human than ever before.

Whenever I'd observed him around Andrei's house or with him, he appeared made of stone. An unbreakable, cold man with no feelings whatsoever.

It seems the Bratva turns men into monsters, but beneath it, many still have hearts. "Thank you, Lyov."

It is nerve-wracking waiting. The silence between the two of us is almost deafening. Our pizza arrives, and it's a welcome distraction for all of twenty minutes.

I keep tapping my foot on the tiled floor, glancing at the clock. Another hour passes, and the door opens.

Roman steps out with blood on his clothes. "He's fine and resting."

I breathe a sigh of relief.

His eyes linger on me. "Vera, he wants to see you."

I glance at Lyov, and he gives me an encouraging nod. My knees shake as I stand to my feet. My stomach is a bundle of nerves as I wonder what he will say.

Will he tell me I'm free to leave? I don't want to leave him, ever.

Andrei is sitting up in the hospital bed. He looks exhausted as his head remains back on a pillow. The moment he sees me, his dark eyes light up. "Vera, come here." He holds his hand out toward me.

I walk toward him and take it, shutting my eyes at the feel of his warm, rough skin against mine.

"You're okay," I breathe.

He chuckles. "Yes, I'm okay." His brow furrows. "Please don't tell me you sat outside this whole time worried?"

I stare at him, wondering whether to answer. "Damn right, I sat outside worried." A man who I've come to adore in such a short space of time was hurt.

I grab his hand and lace my fingers with his. "Roman mentioned the bullet was close to a major artery… I thought—"

He cups my face in his hand, and I stop speaking. "*Krasivaya*, listen."

I stare at him for a moment, waiting for him to speak. We fought side by side and ended my uncle's life. It is over now, and I'm no longer his slave. If he asks me to leave, I won't be able to take the pain.

"You did well today." He smiles. "You're the daughter of a former *pakhan*. A man I respect, even in death. You're not and never have been a slave, Vera." He shakes his head. "As you know, I find the slave trade deplorable."

I can feel the tears prickle my eyes as he speaks. The conversation is heading in only one direction, and I wouldn't say I like it.

"Why are you crying?" he asks, brushing the tears away from my cheeks.

I shake my head, swallowing hard.

"I'm freeing you, but I don't want you to leave, Vera." He pauses a moment, swallowing. "I love you."

The tears fall faster, hearing him say those words as I try to get control of my emotions. It's impossible. They spill like a torrent of waves down my face.

He wipes them away from my face, cupping my chin. "Is it so terrible to be loved by me?"

I shake my head, pain gripping the side of my throat. "No… I-I love you too, Andrei."

He grabs my hand and pulls me onto the edge of the bed, running his hand down my back in a way that sends shivers down my spine. Every little touch from him, no matter the situation, sets me on fire.

"You are so beautiful, Vera." His hand grips the back of my neck possessively, pulling me toward him. I moan as he kisses me hard and deep. "And, so damn insatiable." He smiles against my mouth.

"You shouldn't be kissing me. You should be resting." I pull away and shuffle to a safe distance from him on the hospital bed.

He tries to reach for me, but I shift into the seat next to his bed, crossing one leg over the other. "Are you playing hard to get?" He raises an eyebrow.

"Rest, Andrei," I say, trying to remain serious.

He laughs. "How about I rest, and you ride me?" He pulls back his covers to reveal his tenting boxers.

I can't deny the mere sight of him hard makes my pulse race, but I'm not an idiot. He's just undergone surgery.

"I can see you are considering it," Andrei teases.

"No freaking chance." I cross my arms over my chest. "You need to get some rest. Do you want me to fetch you any food or drink?" I ask, standing up.

Andrei doesn't let up, grabbing my hand and pulling me toward him. I notice him wince at the pressure it puts on his wound. "I'd like you to give me a kiss."

I kiss him softly and chastely, trying to keep him at bay. Andrei won't let me go as he deepens the kiss, demanding entrance with his tongue. "Andrei," I say his name in an attempt at a warning, but it comes out more like a moan.

Roman clears his throat behind us, forcing him to release me. "What the hell do you think you are doing, Andrei?"

I stumble back as he lets go of me. "He wouldn't give in," I say, my cheeks flushing.

Roman chuckles and steps closer. "No, Andrei can be a stubborn as hell bastard."

Andrei's eyes flash. "Watch it. I may be bed-bound for now, but I won't forget you disrespecting me," he growls.

He raises an eyebrow and sighs. "Sorry, sir, I told you to rest up."

The fury on Andrei's features almost scares me. He may be a soft-hearted man beneath it all, but he's also the brutal *pakhan* of the New York brotherhood. I can't ever forget that, even if I want to.

The seriousness cracks, and he smiles. "I know, but I missed Vera." He winks at me before turning cold eyes on his doctor. "But don't speak to me like that again, Roman."

There's still that air of power around him all the time. Even Roman, who seems friendly, fears him. Life would be easier if we were both ordinary people, without the Bratva way of life hanging over our heads.

Many will question Andrei's choice to be with me, considering he purchased me from an auction as a slave, no matter my ancestry.

Roman nods in agreement with his boss's instruction. "Sir. I'm sorry." He bows his head before leaving us alone.

"Why do you act like that?" I ask, tilting my head to the side.

"Like what?"

Will my question annoy him? "You are so harsh and unforgiving to your men."

His brow furrows. "I'm the *pakhan* of my brotherhood. My men have to both fear and respect me." He shakes his head. "If they don't, then I'm risking everything."

I sigh, not understanding the Bratva politics and code they follow. Even though my father was *pakhan*, he kept my siblings and me ignorant. I'm not sure my mom knew much about what he did or who he was when he wasn't with us.

"I don't understand it."

Andrei squeezes my hand. "You will in time, and I intend to keep you around for a very long time."

I smile, thankful that the man I've fallen for loves me too. The other alternative would have been painful.

He regards me. "I know this is an odd time to ask, but are you on any contraceptives?"

My stomach twists, and my eyes widen. *Shit.* When we fucked, I never even considered the consequences. Too caught up in it all. "No, I should have said something. I—"

Andrei grips hold of my chin and pulls me close again. "Good, I want you pregnant with my baby as soon as possible."

His words startle me, and I'm unsure how to feel about them. I'd always wanted to be a mom someday before my family died.

After that, I'd been living on autopilot. Life after killing the man who murdered my family wasn't a consideration.

19

ANDREI

I set the roof up for the evening with the help of Alexi and Lyov. A table with candles lit and rose petals on top. I never trusted my spy before, but Lyov has proved far more reliable than I expected.

Vera has taken a shine to him, which has helped my opinion of him.

Tonight is an important night for both of us. Three months have passed since we killed her uncle. Vera insisted she wanted to kill him, and she did, with my help. I wouldn't say I liked her being involved in ending his life, as she had never killed before.

I had to listen to what she wanted. She found her parents, brother, and sister murdered in the stream that ran through the family home's grounds.

I pull my phone out of my pocket and send off a text to Vera.

Me: Come up to the roof. I'm waiting for you.

It's less than a few seconds before my phone buzzes again.

Vera: I wondered where you were. On my way.

I pace the floor, anxious about seeing her. The door swings open, and she stops still at the sight of me in a suit and the table set up. She's wearing a sexy black silk slip with lace detail. Her face is natural with no makeup, as I like her.

"What's going on?" she asks, glancing around the roof area.

I walk toward her, grabbing her hand and dropping to one knee. "*Krasivaya*, I love you more than anything in this world."

Her eyes turn glossy and wet with tears, and she clutches her hand to her chest.

"I want you to be mine forever." Slipping my hand into my pocket, I pull out the box, housing a simple but large solitaire ring. I flip open the lid and keep my eyes on her emerald jewels as tears trickle down her face. "Will you marry me?" I ask, holding the engagement ring at the end of her ring finger.

She stares at me for a moment, leaving me waiting for most likely only a second, but time moves so slowly at that moment. "Yes," she says, bursting into tears. "I love you, Andrei."

I smile and push the ring onto her finger, jumping

to my feet and lifting her. She giggles as I spin her around before setting her back on her feet.

I rest my hand on the bump of her stomach as she's three months pregnant. It was a shock when I found out I got her pregnant one of the first times we fucked, but it's what I had wanted. "How are you?"

She smiles and closes her hand over mine. "Amazing, I've never been so happy."

I kiss her, but she claws at my neck, deepening the kiss. She is wanton and needy, moaning into my mouth.

When we part, we're both panting, and she's flushed. I glance at the table and the silver platters waiting for us. "Are you ready to eat?" I ask, noticing her nipples are rock hard through her skimpy silk slip.

She shakes her head. "I need you now." She teases her hand down her chest and plays with her nipples, making me lose my mind.

I grab her hand and tug her toward the door she came through. "We'll warm the food up later. There's something I've got to show you."

I lead her downstairs to my room, opening the door and then walking to the bookcase on the far wall. I pull down the book, and the door springs open.

Vera gasps, eyes flashing with curiosity as she steps closer.

I hold out a hand. "Come here."

She walks toward me. Her eyes widen as she takes

in the view in front of her—my pleasure room. "Why did you keep this a secret?"

I shrug. "I've been recovering from my gunshot wound and wasn't up for playing." I grab her hips and dig my fingers into them. "Not to mention, I didn't want to push you too soon," I whisper into her ear.

She licks her bottom lip, and I let her go, watching her walk around the room. She runs her hand across the bondage bench I've longed to see her tied to since we met.

"Do you want to play?" I ask, voice turning husky.

She turns toward me and places her finger against her lips in a playful move. "Hmm... I'm not sure. You might need to convince me."

Challenge accepted.

I step toward her, setting my hands on her hips and pulling her back into me. "Is that right, Miss Popov?" I let my hand roam under her sexy silk slip and pull it up over her hips. "I don't think that will be necessary." I slap her ass in a soft but firm spank, making her jump.

She moans as I grope her other ass cheek before slapping it with the same amount of force. "Andrei," she rasps my name.

"I want to try something," I murmur in her ear.

She bites her bottom lip, glancing back at me. "What?"

I slap her ass again. "No questions. Red is always

the safe word." I pull her slip off over her head and discard it to one side.

Her eyes widen as I lift her off her feet and carry her toward the bench. I set her on her knees, strapping her calves into it first.

A wild, desperate need to have her in this position has plagued me since we met. I fix the straps around her waist before moving to her wrists and tightening those.

She gazes up at me, a mix of fear and desire filling her perfect green eyes. "What are you going to do to me?" Her lips part, and her cheeks flush at the question.

"Wait and see, Printsessa." I grab her chin and press my lips to hers, kissing her hard.

She moans into my mouth as I bite her lip.

I stand behind her momentarily, memorizing the image of my fiancé tied up and spread for me.

Her pussy is dripping wet already. My gaze moves to her perfect, tight asshole, which I've yet to claim. My cock is like steel in my boxer briefs, straining to break free. I step toward her and grope her ass cheeks in my hands.

She shivers, whimpering in anticipation of what I will do to her. The need to paint her ass a perfect red has me spanking her three firm times on each cheek. Her thighs tremble as she gets even wetter.

I repeat the spanking until she's red and panting,

dripping everywhere. My cock is so hard it hurts, but I'm not ready to fuck her yet.

I shift to my knees and part her lips with my tongue, tasting that sweet nectar between her thighs.

"Andrei," she moans my name.

I love making her say my name. I massage her asscheeks as I feast on her arousal. She jolts as my tongue circles her clit, before trailing a path right through her center. I feel her tense as I lick her ass, circling it and then probing at the tight muscles.

"Oh, God…"

I fuck her hole with my tongue, pleasuring her in a way I've longed to do since we met.

She cries out as I slip my fingers into her center while licking her ass. Deep inside of her, the pressure is building already. She's such a good little submissive.

"Andrei, I'm going to—"

I spank her hard, and her body shudders. "No coming until I say so, baby," I groan, gripping her red ass cheeks in my hands.

"Fuck," she says, trying to hold on to the orgasm wanting to explode through her body.

I stop touching her pussy and only tease my tongue over her asshole. The moment her thighs and ass stop shaking, I thrust my fingers back inside of her, and she groans. I love playing with her body like an instrument, strumming her close and stopping so she's teetering on edge.

I pull my fingers from her pussy and circle her

tight, forbidden hole with my finger. Vera tenses. I grab a bottle of lube from under the bench and squirt it on her ass, making her gasp — the need to fuck her there is all-consuming.

My finger slides inside her hole, and she shivers. It's so fucking tight.

"Andrei, what are you—"

I spank her ass, and she gasps. "No questions. Relax and enjoy it," I command.

On my command, she settles down — the tension leaves her shoulders and back. I add more lube to her ass and slip another finger inside of her.

My cock is leaking into my pants at the thought of stretching her hole with my dick. "Do you like that, *Krasivaya?*"

She nods her head, muttering incoherent words in response.

I spank her ass with my free hand. "Answer me."

"Yes, sir," she cries out, shuddering again.

She's on the edge of coming undone, but I haven't given her permission yet.

"Andrei, please, I need to—"

I spank her ass again and utter the three words she's been longing to hear, "Come for me."

It's intense and powerful as I keep fingering her asshole. Her body shudders and shakes as much as the bench restraints will allow.

I slip a third finger inside her hole as she loosens up, allowing the invasion more freely. I pull my fingers out of her and move around to her face, unzipping my pants and pulling them off.

Vera stares at me with wide eyes, cheeks pink, and eyes glassy and unfocused. *Damn.* She looks like a masterpiece.

She licks her lips as I pull my boxers down, letting my cock spring to attention in front of her. My cock is an inch too far away from her. Vera tries desperately to reach it, sticking her tongue out toward the tip. It's a sexy as fuck image I store in my mind.

"Do you want to suck your fiancé's cock?"

She nods her head, keeping her tongue outstretched.

"Open wide."

She does as I say, and I push my cock into her mouth, groaning at the warm, wet feel of her tongue on the underside of me. Hot splashes of pearly cum drip from the tip all over her tongue, and she hums, closing her lips around my shaft.

I grab her hair tight and ram my cock deep into her throat, loving the way she relaxes and breathes through her nose. The wet sound of my cock fucking her throat drives me insane as I let every inch slide inside of her, holding her nose against my lower abdomen.

She gags, and I let go, saliva dripping all over my cock and the bench. Tears prickle in her eyes as she comes back for me, opening her mouth. This woman is too fucking perfect.

I slide inside of her throat again, letting her swallow my cock and my leaking seed. She devours my cock as though she's starving for me. Her body is bending to my will.

She moans in protest as I remove my cock from her mouth and step away. I bend down and kiss her, tangling my tongue with hers. "It's time for me to be inside of you."

Her eyes light up with a hot need that makes my balls clench. I move to stand behind her and line myself up with her soaking wet pussy. She gasps as I thrust deep inside her perfect cunt, loving the way she grips me so tightly.

It's as if she never wants to let me leave her body. I grunt as I thrust in and out of her. Fucking her hard and fast the way she always loves it. Her body bends to my will. I slap her already red ass, making her body quiver and shake.

"Oh God," she screams, coming undone on my cock so hard I can hardly hold on, but I have to.

I pull out of her center and undo the straps on her legs, waist, and arms. She stays still as I lift her and carry her to the bed in the center. Her hands tease over the waterproof bedding as I tie the straps around her legs and wrists. My spreader bar is stowed at the side of the bed, and I grab it, fixing it to her legs.

Her eyes go wide as she realizes she can't clamp her thighs shut at all. "Oh…"

"I'm going to fuck your ass," I say, fisting my cock

and coating it in lube. I squeeze some onto Vera's hole, which is perfectly angled at me by the spreader bar. "Relax," I mutter, leaning down to kiss her hard and long. My cock resting on her twitching prepared hole.

"Fuck my ass, Andrei," she moans, writhing beneath me.

I groan into her mouth and sit back on my haunches, lining my cock up with her puckered hole. The spreader bar keeps it angled toward me, and her pussy is stretched and dripping. An image I've only imagined in my wildest fantasies since the day we first met.

I press my cock into her, and her tight as fuck hole stretches around the throbbing head. "Fuck," I mutter, shutting my eyes and trying to prepare myself for how tight she will be.

My hands claw at her thighs as I push harder, sinking inch after inch into her. She moans, lips open and eyes fluttering shut.

"Look at me, Vera," I command.

Her eyes shoot open, meeting my gaze with such heat I nearly shoot every drop of seed into her. I grit my teeth, sinking so far that my balls rest against her skin.

She whimpers, and her thighs shake. "Fuck me, Andrei," she rasps, voice a different, husky tone.

I give her time to get used to the new sensation, fucking her slowly. Her head falls back onto the bench as she watches my cock sink in and out of her tight hole.

"Damn, you are so tight," I groan, teasing her clit between my finger and thumb.

"It's so good," she gasps, eyes clamping shut.

I slap her thigh. "Look at me while I fuck your ass," I command.

Her deep emerald eyes flick open and meet mine. "Fuck my ass, Andrei, please," she begs.

Her begging sets the beast inside of me loose. I roar and buck my hips, thrusting in and out of her tight hole with fierce abandon. "Mine, forever," I growl, gazing at the beautiful creature spread and bound for me.

My cock sinks in and out of her tight, puckered hole as she moans and flushes an even deeper red.

"So full, so good," she mutters.

My fingers tease her clit again, and she will come again. I love how well she comes and how easily I can command her orgasms.

"I want you to come while I'm balls deep in your ass," I growl, slapping her thighs and driving into her with all the passion, love, and fury hitting me at that moment.

My pregnant fiancé is spread for me, allowing me to fuck the most intimate, forbidden part of her body.

"Fuck, I'm going to come," she cries, eyes

clamping shut under the sheer pressure of the orgasm rushing for her.

"Eyes open," I command.

She does as I say, eyes dilated with such pleasure. I'm on the edge of coming undone myself. "I want to look into your eyes as you come with my cock in your ass."

"Fuck." Her body convulses, and her hold tightens around my dick, making it impossible not to come undone.

I shoot my load deep inside her as she orgasms. We are both breathless and panting as I keep moving my cock in and out of her until I'm sure my balls are drained and she has returned to earth.

I slip out of her and pull her into my chest, holding her close. A few moments of perfect silence fall between us before she interrupts it. "I don't under-stand why we haven't been in this room before," she says.

I chuckle, entwining my fingers with hers and bringing them to my mouth. I press a kiss against them. "Good things come to those who wait."

She yawns. "I can't wait to do that again."

My cock twitches in excitement. We are not leaving this room tonight.

20

EPILOGUE

VERA

*T*wo years later…

The expanse of the ocean stretches out before me as I sit on the small cove beach on the soft, white sand. The pink rays of the sun are peaking over the horizon, painting the sky a fabulous watercolor of pastel pink and yellow against the darkness of dusk.

I feel like I'm staring at a masterpiece of art. Saint Lucia is the most stunning place I've ever visited. I never liked the seaside, but I could get used to waking up here *every* morning.

When I lost my family, I couldn't sleep without waking from terrible nightmares. Five years on, and It's getting easier because of one man.

"You are up early, Printsessa," Andrei says behind me, always calling me Princess in Russian to this day. Although, I'm not the only girl he calls princess anymore.

"I had to see the sunrise." I turn and smile at the love of my life, walking toward me in his boxer briefs. A man I can't imagine life without anymore. "Is she sleeping?"

He sits down by my side, setting his hand on the small of my back. "Yes, and Elena is in the next room if she wakes." He sets a kiss on my forehead. "You worry too much."

Amelia, our daughter, is one and a half years old now. He's right. I do worry too much. I never knew how scary it would be to love someone as much as our daughter or Andrei.

After losing everyone that mattered to me, I've got people to lose again. Elena is our nanny who helps out at night to ensure Amelia sleeps, and we do, too.

With Andrei's involvement in such a dangerous, crime-ridden world, we'll always be in danger. "I can't help it."

He sets his hand on my bloated belly, kissing my cheek. "Has he been kicking this morning?"

"A little… I think he's almost ready to come out." I wish he were, as being pregnant is no picnic.

Andrei shakes his head. "I want him to be born on American soil, not in Saint Lucia."

I smirk at that. "We still have three months until I'm due."

"How about an early morning swim?"

I glance at my husband, tilting my head to the side. His eyes are full of hot desire. Ever since he got me pregnant for the second time, he's been more insatiable than ever. I bite my bottom lip. "I haven't got a swimsuit."

His eyes flash, and he growls. "Good, I want you naked." I glance down and notice the hard length of him pressing against his tight boxer briefs.

I lick my bottom lip before jumping to my feet.

He watches me as I pull my nightdress over my head, revealing my naked body and rounded belly. I turn around and walk backward toward the sea. His eyes darken as I walk away without a word.

I can sense him following me as I turn and walk into the water. The waves crash over my feet, and I sigh as it cools them. Since I've been pregnant, I'm always hot, and my feet always ache. Not to mention, the temperature here hasn't fallen below seventy-seven degrees since we arrived.

A pair of strong arms wrap around my lower abdomen beneath my baby bump, and he kisses the back of my neck. His hard, thick cock rests between my legs, making me wet and needy in an instant. "So fucking beautiful," he groans against my skin.

He walks me further into the ocean until the water covers my swollen belly. My nipples are hard peaks as he forces us both into the tepid embrace of the ocean. I turn and wrap my arms around his neck and my legs around his waist.

The water holds me up as his cock teases between my thighs. I moan, arching my back and enjoying the intimate feel of him behind me in the water. It's so natural.

"I'm going to fuck you, Printsessa," he murmurs into my ear, sucking on my earlobe.

"Yes, Andrei, fuck me."

He groans, sliding his hands onto my hips and guiding the tip of his cock to my entrance.

I wait, expecting him to thrust every inch deep and hard. Instead, he teases his cock over my clit, bumping the thick head over and over it again and again. We're the only two people in this world while on the private beach below our villa up on the hill.

"Tease," I murmur.

He bites my bottom lip hard enough to hurt. "You love it." His fingertips claw into my ass hard enough to mark me.

I gasp as he sucks on my tongue and then bites at it. He finds any way to make me feel that pain, which sets me on fire and turns me to jelly in his arms all at once.

Without warning, he thrusts into me. His cock is as deep as it can go with one pump of his hips.

My head falls back, and I moan, loving the way he stretches me. He sinks his teeth into my collarbone as he lifts me up and down his shaft in the water. His powerful legs anchored to the sea bed.

"You are so fucking tight," he groans, fucking me slow and hard.

I groan with every thrust, clawing onto his shoulders, bouncing up and down his cock faster.

"I'm in control," he growls, grabbing my hips hard and making me still on his cock.

"Yes, sir," I moan, kissing him. The fire inside of me roaring and burning so brightly I know it will never go out. Even as time passes, it does not extinguish my burning passion for this man.

He sucks on my tongue, warring for control and pushing me to submit. "How did I get so lucky?" he asks, groaning into my mouth.

It's a question I ask myself every day. How did I get so lucky to find a man who loves me so hard?

I ease my grip on his shoulders and allow him to take me, submitting to him. He loves the initial struggle as he subdues me, forcing me to bend to his will.

There's something so satisfying, letting him take control when we make love. He makes me feel desired and wanted — the animalistic way he takes me.

I bite my lip as he reaches between our bodies and rubs my clit, making me shiver. "Fuck," I groan, clawing at his shoulders again.

The sun is rising over the water, spreading speckles of light across the ocean. Andrei's tanned skin looks almost golden as the sunrise lights his face.

Who knew love could be this good?

He carries me toward the cove's edge and rests on a rock under the water. I gasp as he slips out of me and then nudges at my back entrance with his cock. "Andrei, we don't have any lube."

He grunts, sliding his fingers inside of me and spreading my juices into my ass. I groan as he fingers my ass, trying to get me ready. There's a fire in his eyes. He's lost control, and no matter what I say, he's going there—a dominant male who would never hurt me but can lose control of his urges.

"Fuck, Andrei," I say as he slides three thick fingers into my asshole, filling me with a different pleasure.

"Don't worry. I'm not going to fuck you in the ass." He bites on the lobe of my ear. "I just want to finger it while I fuck you," he grunts, pulling me onto his lap. The hard length of him strains against my center, making me wild.

His huge, thick cock rests at my entrance. He slides in, filling me so completely — his fingers in my asshole and his cock in my pussy. "Ride me," he growls.

I do as he says, riding his length while he keeps three fingers lodged deep in my ass. It's a thrilling sensation that sends me racing for the edge so fast. He sucks on my nipples as I rise and fall. So many sensations I can't register them all in my mind as they merge into heavenly bliss.

The man knows how to pull my orgasms from me easier than breathing, working me to a crescendo. It blurs my vision as I drive myself up and down him harder and faster. His fingers are still dipping in and out of my ass.

"Fuck, Andrei," I moan, forcing my lips to his and delving inside his mouth with a crazed need.

His hard cock is pulsing and throbbing inside of me as he pounds deep. Every thrust hitting the spot inside of me sends me to heaven. Anytime he's inside of me is heaven. I wish I could live like this, filled and stretched with him.

Each thrust of his cock drives me higher, and every time he moves his fingers in and out of my ass, the pleasure heightens. I groan as heat floods me, and the desperate need to tumble over the edge claws at me.

Andrei pulls his fingers from my hole and teases my nipple instead, sucking on the other one at the same time.

"Fuck, I'm going to come," I cry, rising and falling harder and faster on his length.

He keeps sucking and nipping at my hard nipples, making me insane. I clamp down around him. The hot, raging fire of an orgasm slams into me hard and fast. He grabs hold of my ass cheeks possessively and pounds into me even harder and faster, fucking me right through it.

He bites my collarbone and grunts like an animal as he shoots his seed deep inside of me, marking me as he always does. We're panting and breathless.

Andrei remains on the rock in the sea as the waves crash around us.

His dark eyes are burning with such love and desire that it makes my chest swell. "You are so fucking perfect," he mutters, sliding his hand behind my neck and kissing me with such tenderness. It's a contrast to the wild way he fucked me a moment ago.

"Printsessa," Andrei mutters, resting his forehead against mine and breathing against my lips.

The pain of my past is being washed away with the waves that encase us. We are healing and mending each other as each day goes by. Andrei gives me a reason to live. Life is no longer about revenge. It's about building a family with the man whose lap I'm sitting on.

I will always be his Printsessa, and he will forever be my savior.

———

THANK you for reading Bought by the Bratva, the first book in The Bratva Brotherhood series. I hope you enjoyed following Andrei & Vera's story.

The next book follows his spy, Lyov, and is available through Kindle Unlimited or to buy on Amazon.

<u>Captured: A Dark Mafia Romance</u>

There's a war raging, and I'm caught in the middle.

My father has had a run-in with the New York Brotherhood, and one of the New York Brotherhood spies takes me.

Lyov is muscle-bound, tattooed, and gorgeous.

He is also quiet and brooding.

He won't speak to me.

He barely looks at me.

On the rare occasions, I catch his eyes on me, they're burning with dark desire.

I have to escape. Otherwise, I'll end up as collateral damage.

So, why do I want to stay? Even more so when he touches me.

I can't ignore the way this man makes me feel.

We're from two opposing sides, and I know it can't work.

Our attraction could lead to destruction, but my heart doesn't want to give up.

Captured by the Bratva is the second book in the Bratva Brotherhood series. It's a safe story with no cliffhangers, a HEA, and no cheating. This story has hot scenes, some dark themes, and bad language. Like most of my books, it features an over-the-top possessive alpha male.

ALSO BY BIANCA COLE

Once Upon a Villian

Pride: A Dark Arranged Marriage Romance

Hook: A Dark Forced Marriage Mafia Romance

Wicked: A Dark Forbidden Mafia Romance

Unhinged: A Dark Captive Cartel Romance

The Syndicate Academy

Corrupt Educator: A Dark Forbidden Mafia Academy Romance

Cruel Bully: A Dark Mafia Academy Romance

Sinful Lessons: A Dark Forbidden Mafia Academy Romance

Playing Dirty: A Dark Enemies to Lovers Forbidden Mafia Academy Romance

Chicago Mafia Dons

Merciless Defender: A Dark Forbidden Mafia Romance

Violent Leader: A Dark Enemies to Lovers Captive Mafia Romance

Evil Prince: A Dark Arranged Marriage Romance

Brutal Daddy: A Dark Captive Mafia Romance

Cruel Vows: A Dark Forced Marriage Mafia Romance

Dirty Secret: A Dark Enemies to Loves Mafia Romance

Dark Crown: A Dark Arranged Marriage Romance

Boston Mafia Dons Series

Empire of Carnage: A Dark Captive Mafia Romance

Cruel Daddy: A Dark Mafia Arranged Marriage Romance

Savage Daddy: A Dark Captive Mafia Roamnce

Ruthless Daddy: A Dark Forbidden Mafia Romance

Vicious Daddy: A Dark Brother's Best Friend Mafia Romance

Wicked Daddy: A Dark Captive Mafia Romance

New York Mafia Doms Series

Her Irish Daddy: A Dark Mafia Romance

Her Russian Daddy: A Dark Mafia Romance

Her Italian Daddy: A Dark Mafia Romance

Her Cartel Daddy: A Dark Mafia Romance

Romano Mafia Brother's Series

Her Mafia Daddy: A Dark Daddy Romance

Her Mafia Boss: A Dark Romance

Her Mafia King: A Dark Romance

New York Brotherhood Series

Bought: A Dark Mafia Romance

Captured: A Dark Mafia Romance

Claimed: A Dark Mafia Romance

Bound: A Dark Mafia Romance

Taken: A Dark Mafia Romance

Forbidden Series

Bryson: An Enemies to Lovers Office Romance

Logan: A First Time Professor And Student Romance

Ryder: An Enemies to Lovers Office Romance

Dr Fox: A Fordbidden Romance

Royally Mated Series

Her Faerie King: A Faerie Royalty Paranormal Romance

Her Alpha King: A Royal Wolf Shifter Paranormal
Romance

Her Dragon King: A Dragon Shifter Paranormal Romance

Her Vampire King: A Dark Vampire Romance

ABOUT THE AUTHOR

I love to write stories about over the top alpha bad boys who have heart beneath it all, fiery heroines, and happily-ever-after endings with heart and heat. My stories have twists and turns that will keep you flipping the pages and heat to set your kindle on fire.

For as long as I can remember, I've been a sucker for a good romance story. I've always loved to read. Suddenly, I realized why not combine my love of two things, books and romance?

My love of writing has grown over the past four years and I now publish on Amazon exclusively, weaving stories about dirty mafia bad boys and the women they fall head over heels in love with.

If you enjoyed this book please follow her on Amazon, Bookbub or any of the below social media platforms for alerts when more books are released.

Printed in Great Britain
by Amazon